The Legend of V

Book 3
Psycho Star Showdown

by Varak Kaloustian

CONTENTS

Chapter 1

FIRE! FIRE!

I t's the last day of school, there are five minutes left on the clock, and you've got no plans ahead of you for the summer. Your body relaxes in your stiff chair as the cool breeze from outside makes your hair sway.

That's essentially how I feel right now... all the time. And it's great.

My name is V. I have big, dark-brown eyes, I'm 5′ 10″, and rock a fluffy, brown Afro. My outfit reflects my mood, as I'm wearing a torn white shirt and sport shorts. I couldn't be more excited because in a few days I'll be 14. Everyone typically always enjoys their birthday, but I especially enjoy mine because my friends set it up. Ever since we were about 10 or so, we decided to plan birthdays for each other. Why? Let's just say it involved a clown, a marching band, and a whoopee cushion.

Now, back to my more engaging matter. "C'mon, Sonic! Just a little more, buddy. One more level and we'll finally take out Eggman, and all the forest animals will be free! Until the next game, anyway."

"V, can you take out the trash, dear?" My mom calls from the bottom of the tree house we live in.

"Five minutes, mom! I'm about to take out Eggman."

"Who?"

"Never mind."

– *Dark Spirit, can You go take out the trash?*

– *Why should I complete your petty chores? It doesn't look like you're doing anything significant right now.*

– *I beg to differ! The fate of South Island depends on it.*

1

– Very well. One moment.

I should explain how I just telepathically communicated with a spirit living inside me. See, this is the Dark Spirit, an age-old divine entity that helped me save the galaxy, twice.

"V! Why is the trash floating?" My mom is not happy.

"The important thing is that it's being dealt with, right?"

"I agree." Z, my older brother, concurs from outside, while practicing chipping onto a small putting green.

"Yes! Finally. Take that, Eggman." I place my controller down in triumph.

"The trash is taken care of, V." The Dark Spirit, in Its phoenix form, hovers back into my body.

"Thanks. And the residents of South Island are safe also."

"Thank Heavens."

Just then, one of my two best pals, Griff, flies in through the window. He has about the same build as me, except his hair is blond and completely straight. Right now, he's wearing a plain dark-blue T-shirt with gray sport shorts. "We've got trouble, V. A fire broke out near Sacramento."

"Well, what are we supposed to do about it?"

"Did you forget? The police tasked us to help put out natural disasters."

"Oh, right. I forgot about that." Well, there goes my feeling of relaxation. "In my defense, that was issued a while ago."

"That's fair, but that doesn't matter right now. Let's go!"

"Right behind you, buddy."

You're probably asking yourself why two tweens are chasing a fire with the intent of putting it out. Well, to put it simply, Griff and I have amazing powers. In our past adventures, we discovered The Legend of V, a legacy bequeathed to me to destroy the Unbound Evil when It inevitably returns. To combat the Unbound Evil, we met the Dark Spirit and the Solar and Shadow Prophecies, two sets of five super-powered tablets that bestow an elevated state of being to anything that comes in contact with them. With one set of prophecies, you acquire an extreme form, but with two, you get a chaos form. Once you experience the prophecies, you can even harness their power without being in an extreme or chaos form, and that's exactly what Griff and I are doing now, to get to Sacramento from San Francisco in under a minute.

"WOOOHOOO!" Griff does a backflip while zooming through the air.

"It's good to be back in action. So, where's the fi– oh." A monstrous blaze is burning away massive amounts of farmland and is only increasing by the second. Griff and I look at each other, nod, and close our eyes, focusing on our inner strength. Wisdom… speed… power… chaos… solar… We open our eyes and burst into our extreme forms.

Griff's eyes turn yellow, and his hair and hands burst orange flames. My eyes and hair radiate the sun's colors, my hair goes berserk.

"You get the right side of the flames, V. I'll get the left."

"Sounds like a plan."

We both face our hands at the flames and squint. As we do so, the flames pour into our hands and our bodies absorb the inferno's power. In no time at all, the flame ceases and the remaining farmland is spared.

"High five, V!" As I run back to Griff, we both leap at each other and smack our right hands together so profoundly that the surviving grasses dance.

"So now that the day is saved, what next?"

"How about some In-N-Out?" Griff suggests.

"Ohhhh. Good call. Okay, let's head back."

Our extreme forms subside, and we take to the skies once more. "By the way, V," Griff starts, "where did Azilez go? I haven't seen her at all today."

"She said something about shopping for my birthday-cake ingredients. I didn't want to go with her. You know how long that could take."

Chapter 2
Carry On, Wayward Rainbow Girl
- AZILEZ -

It feels SO good to shop again! Helping Vizor find his memories a month ago really drained me. I'm glad I can finally just skip around the different stores in downtown San Francisco and look for food again. I absolutely adore food. I love eating it, smelling it, buying it, and, above all, making it. I'm a culinary master, if I do say so myself. I can make crab cakes from scratch! But that's not what I'm hunting down ingredients for today.

"Ma'am?"

I'm out shopping for the perfect red-velvet-cake ingredients for V's 14th birthday. I always make the cakes for birthdays. Even my own. Though my mom, Candice, always tries stopping me for mine and fails every time. Tee hee!

"Excuse me. Ma'am."

Okay, let's check the list to make sure I have everything before I head back. Milk, flower, sugar, eggs, butter...

"MA'AM!"

"Huh? What? Where?" Uh oh. Did I doze off for too long?

"You're holding up the line."

Oh, shoot! I am. Everyone behind me does NOT look happy. Grinding teeth, tapping feet, and, yeesh, that stare isn't welcoming.

"Sorry, everyone! I'll leave now." I didn't mean to make everyone wait so long... doh! I feel like a dolt now! Better not tell V or Griff that this happened. Maybe it's a good thing V decided not to come with me.

Anyway, where was I? Oh, right! The list. Hmm… let's see. Milk? Check. Flower? It's there. Sugar? Mmhmm. Vinegar? Yup. Baking soda? Tiny, but, yeah, it's there. Cocoa powder? No! Right, I didn't get that because I wanted to specifically get it from the Ghirardelli Chocolate Company's factory.

Also, I just realized I have a lot of bags to carry. I know it sounds like I shouldn't because I only listed off, like, five ingredients, but I plan on making this cake HUGE. So… oh! I know. I'll use my trusty paint-brush to summon forth a bunch of boxes for the bags to be placed in. That way, when I fly to Ghirardelli, the ingredients won't move around so much. Yeah! I like the sound of that.

Okay, since that's done, time for Ghirardelli. Now, to just summon a rainbow board for me to ride on… There we go! All set. Prepare for liftoff. "WHEEEE!" I get lost in the fog and mist of the early San Francisco morning, and pop out right as I get to Ghirardelli Square.

"*snnniiiffff* Ahhh… it always smells euphoric here."

"I think you say that every time you walk anywhere near here, Azilez. Haha!"

"Oh, Bessie. Hi, there. Giving out samples today?" Bessie works here at Ghirardelli Square. She sees me pretty much every time I come here, and trust me when I say that's a lot. Anyway, she typically passes out samples of milk chocolate filled with luscious caramel to pedestrians with a jolly smile on her face. It complements her abundance of freckles and cherry-red, wavy hair.

"No. Working the shop today, actually. Just out here to get some air."

"Oh, perfect. I actually need cocoa powder. You mind helping me with the transaction?"

"But I'm on break…"

"Thanks, Bessie!"

"Ehh. I shouldn't have expected anything less from her." Bessie begrudgingly follows behind me into the cute floral-covered shack next to the main chocolate factory.

"Let's see…"

"Which can would you like, Azilez? Sweetened or unsweetened?" Bessie nestles herself on a chair behind the register.

"Uh… let's go with unsweetened. There's already gonna be a TON of sugar in this cake."

"Good choice! That'll be $17.50."

"Here you a–" OWW! My leg! What… was that? Mrrrrgg…*thud*

"Azilez! AZILEZ!"

"Target has been captured. Returning to the White House, immediately."

Chapter 3

Trumboozle Bamboozlement

Well, now that the fire is out and my tummy is satisfied, it's time to kick back and relax again. "Hey, everyone, Griff and I are back."

"V! Yay, you're home! Come watch SpongeBob with me." My little brother, D, runs up to me and tugs my already tattered shirt.

"Okay, okay. Sure. Griff, care to join us?"

"Sure. I don't have anything else to do today."

The three of us make ourselves comfortable in the living-room couch, with D sitting in the middle, Griff on the right, and me on the left. D picks up the blocky TV remote and clicks the power button. He then switches the TV's mode to DVR.

"Which episode do you want to watch today, D?"

"Well… how about the original SpongeBob movie?"

Griff and I look at each other. He shrugs as if to say "why not." I give D a thumbs-up, and his eyes twinkle. He loves the *SpongeBob SquarePants* movie. He first watched it a month ago and has been hooked since. I can't really blame him. It's my favorite movie too. Ever since Griff and I were kids, we'd always watch it after school together, back when Rodger took care of us.

D jumps from the couch and hurries into the kitchen. He climbs on a stool and takes out a bag of microwavable popcorn from the top of the pantry. Then we hear this:

"Ahhhh! Heeeeeelp, V, Griff!" We rush to the kitchen. He's not in here! "WOAH!" Outside, we hear a very distinct noise: a rattling paintbrush. That's Azilez! Is she in trouble too?

Only one way to find out. We burst through the front door and jump out to the yard below. There, we see only Azilez and D, though D is shaking for some reason. "Uh... what's the matter, D? It's just Azilez."

"She threw me out of the open window!"

Azilez? Throwing D with the intent to harm him? I don't buy it...

– *And neither do I. 'Azilez' is missing a soul.*

– *Then who do You suppose is in front of us, Dark Spirit? Griff?*

– *Dunno, V. But let's deal with this aggressive fake first!*

"Azilez?"

"Hi, guys!" She turns around, with her crystal brown eyes and radiant smile. She doesn't seem or sound too different. So that rules out the Unbound Evil and her evil side. What could have happened to her, then?

"Now, D. Be a sweetie and come with me." Her left hand transforms into a metal butterfly net and encloses D. Well, I think we can safely say she's a robot.

– *Griff, get D out of there. The Dark Spirit and I will handle Azilez.*

– *Sounds good. You go left. I'll go right.*

Griff jumps in front of Azilez, attempting to confront her. She focuses on him. Though if this clone is based off the actual Azilez, that won't last for long.

Watch this. "Hey, Azilez! Your art sucks."

"WHO SAID THAT?" Reeled in like a fish. The moment she turns around, Griff uses his hammer fists to break the net and sets D free. "OW! Griff, that's not very nice."

"Now, V!"

"Huh?"

The Dark Spirit and I combine to form Dark V. I slip through the robot's metal exterior and destroy the internal battery. I pop out in front of Azilez, right next to Griff and D, with my dark-purple eyes and protruding straight hairline covering my right eye. The robot clone falls over, literally dead on the inside. I begin to inspect it. "Hmm..."

"What is it?" D asks.

"Well, I'm just wondering who would make a robot clone of

Azilez?" The Dark Spirit and I return to normal.

"V! GRIFF! D! GET IN HERE, RIGHT NOW!" Uh oh. That screech. Only Candice can scratch nails on a chalkboard that effortlessly.

"Yes, ma'am!" None of us dawdle, and head straight back into the tree house.

Inside, the TV is turned on, and it's playing the news. "What did you need, Candice?" As if Griff doesn't already know. It just looked like we killed her daughter.

"WHY IS MY DAUGHTER IN A PRISON CELL?"

That escalated quickly… WHAT? "Whoa, whoa, whoa, slow down. A prison cell? Where did you hear this?"

Candice calms down a little. "Listen to this!" She rewinds the interview with the new president of the United States, Trumboozle, to its starting point.

"I promised, in my campaign, to deport all freaks and mutants that have been repeatedly causing chaos all over the world. And now, we have one of them behind bars. Big bars. Beautiful bars. Those bars will hold her good, believe me."

The crowd cheers, as the picture on the screen changes to a shackled Azilez, wearing a bright-orange prison getup. "HEY! HEY! WE HAVEN'T DONE A THING. IF ANYTHING, THIS WORLD WOULD BE GONE WITHOUT US!"

The picture then cuts back to Trumboozle and the roaring sound of mixed applause and boos. You know, if you look hard enough, I bet you can see the egg he blends into his hair every morning. I mean, how else does he get his hair that yellow?

In case that insult didn't clue you in yet, I absolutely despise this guy. Not only did he somehow get to be president, but he also vowed to get rid of the very beings that saved the world… twice. If that doesn't scream incompetence, I don't know what does.

"I think he has a very noble cause. Being able to take such initiative to protect this country. He truly will go down in history as a great president." The only voice more incompetent than Trumboozle himself is the media that supports him. His posse not only blindly supports his ridiculous platform, but they're too scared to oppose him for some reason. It'd be like if I never stood up to the Unbound Evil the first time. Our world would be destroyed. Except this time it might actually happen.

"WELL, IS ANYONE GONNA EXPLAIN WHAT SHE DID TO DESTROY THE WORLD OR WHAT?" Candice has her fists on her hips.

"Look, Azilez didn't do anything. Trumboozle is referring to the two times we saved the world, and likely the ruckus that we caused in Cairo with King Tut. Azilez wasn't even there when that happened! She only joined us for our second mission to stop the Unbound Evil."

Griff and D become less intimidated. "That's right! So whatever Azilez's predicament is don't worry about it. V, D, and I will set her free."

"That's what I like to hear!" With all this yelling, Candice sounds like an army instructor. "Now mooooove out!"

D grabs his pickaxe from upstairs, and we make our way to Washington, DC, to save Azilez. Although, with national security on our tail, it's probably best that we travel unnoticed. Though that's kind of hard when you have the ability to travel at the speed of light.

"Hey, guys?"

"Yeah, V?" D turns around, giant brown eyes melting my heart away.

"We should probably go to Suicide Cliff, descend to the beach below, and enter DC through the ocean. Trumboozle's security forces could prove to be a nuisance."

"Good call." Griff leads the way to the abandoned pier site on the outer edge of downtown San Francisco. I heard this place shut down after a death about ten years ago. There were no bars to prevent people from falling off the edge, so after a single death was reported, the entire area was shut off to the public. But, since Trumboozle believes we're mutant freaks, I guess we'll make the exception and say we're NOT a part of the public. Just in case there's security around.

"Hey, guys. Hold my hands."

"What for?" Griff asks.

"I'm going to have the Dark Spirit make us invisible. We don't want to get spotted in an abandoned pier, do we?"

"I guess not. C'mon, D. Hold his other hand."

Our hands touch, and the Dark Spirit courses through all of us. We jump down from the top of the cliff, since our powers and the Dark Spirit's will negate any damage the impact would deal.

"All right, let's zoom to DC!"

"Wait, V!"

"Did you forget something?"

"No, no. It's just that 'zoom' part. If we travel too fast, won't we blow our cover?"

That's actually a great point. Griff's right. "Yeah, we can tone down the speed a little. Let's say... to 500 miles per hour. That way, we won't break the sound barrier."

"Good. Now we're ready!"

"So this is DC? It's a lot smellier than I thought it'd be." D nearly faints from the abysmal trash odor.

"That's because we're in a back alley." Griff picks him up off the cold, damp pavement.

"Dark Spirit? Can You sense Azilez from here?" I ask.

"I'll try. Griff, assist Me. Your sensory powers, too, are strong."

"Sure." Griff closes his eyes and places his right index finger on his forehead. Deep in thought, he makes a slight humming noise like he's some sort of human radar. "Bingo! Found her."

"Likewise." The Dark Spirit follows.

"Well? Don't keep us in suspense. Where is she?" I cover my nose.

"A site somewhere in the outskirts of the city. If we get close, I'll know which building for sure."

"Okay, buddy. Just point in the general direction, and we'll start booking it."

With all of us holding hands again, Griff sidesteps out of trash hell and points to the direction opposite from which we came.

"Okay, guys. Hang on tight!" I jump up to the rooftops of the city in order to avoid any pedestrians. From there, I moon-bounce from building to building, careful to make sure I don't break or knock over anything.

After a few minutes pass by, Griff barks, "Stop!" I jump down to the ground, and Griff, once again, places his right index finger on his forehead. "That one. Right in front of us." Griff points to an abandoned, dilapidated factory. It looks like this place hasn't been used in years, considering most of the building has rusted off.

"Call me skeptical, but I don't think anything like a cyborg can be made here. Are you sure this is the place?"

"I should be a little more specific. She's UNDER the building, not in it."

"Oh." It makes sense, now that I think about it. Imagine if they were cloning humans and someone just accidentally walked in, mistaking it for a common office building or something. That'd be a story for the ages.

"C'mon, you guys! Who knows what that awful president is doing to her?"

"Right." The three of us walk into the site, careful not to detach hands. Griff and D look around at the ruined architecture, avoiding anything that might make a creaking sound. I begin to think about the current predicament, and wonder how the government could catch Azilez. It's not like it's easy to fight her. She has the prophecies' powers and a brush that can materialize literally anything.

Regardless of how they caught her, I'm just going to get her out of there and expose Trumboozle's malicious nature. I mean, sending a cyborg of one of my two best friends to attack and destroy my little brother? I won't let that slide.

"Hey, guys! I found an elevator."

"Nice job, D." Griff nods. He walks up and lifts his right finger to press the elevator's down arrow. Wait…

"Griff! That might be protected by an–" BBBRRRRIINNNGGG! BBBRRRRIINNNGGG! "… alarm."

"Well, there goes our cover." Griff turns around, scratching the back of his head. He blushes a little out of embarrassment.

"Don't worry. We'll just have to blitz the place, then!" I burst into my extreme form and break down the elevator door. Since I clearly don't have a government ID on me, I'm forced to break the elevator's floor too. Griff and D also go extreme and follow me. D's extreme form has his pickaxe catch fire. His hair glows green and flies around like grass ejecting from a lawn mower.

Inside the research facility, we're met by a siege of armed guards. They immediately fire at us. It's no use, though. We fly faster than their bullets and end up behind them. D slashes his pickaxe, letting out a flame burst that sends all the soldiers into the walls. "Sorry, but we're on a mission." D snaps his fingers and catches up to Griff and me.

We make it to the core of the facility. To our distaste, we're met by the big man himself: Trumboozle.

"Well, well. I am so very honored to be in your presence, chosen son."

"Chosen son? No, it's chosen o–"

"Wrong. Not according to… an article I just saw."

"That's pretty flimsy evidence."

"Well, so is your reputation. Because you have done nothing to keep this world out of harm's way!"

Can I even be mad at a person's judgment when I know it's wrong? No, not really. What I can be mad about is that he's using this slander to tarnish my good name! Not just mine, but Griff's, D's, Azilez's… He's going to be the end of all of us if I just keep letting him talk. "You're real lucky I'm in a good mood today. Tell you what. You release Azilez, and I'll forget you even tried to deport us. Deal?"

"Do I look stupid to you?" He squints his eyes down even further than he normally would and twists his hands face up.

"Do you want the politically-correct answer? Or the right answer?"

"I hate being politically correct! This country needs a strong leader in order to–"

"Never mind. Forget it." I just can't win with this guy.

"Deal with little pests like you!" Suddenly, a tremor breaks out. The ground parts, and a giant mechanical suit encloses Trumboozle, complete with a missile cannon, jet boosters, a protective shield, and…

A GIANT METAL PAINBRUSH? That's it! "Didn't expect that, did you? Your little girlfriend's powers have proven quite useful."

Azilez? My girlfriend? No way. I couldn't. Just end me now. Nrrgh! I'm getting off topic. "What have you done to her?"

"All you need to know is that her powers fuel this suit. As long as I have her powers protecting me, you can't do a thing to me."

"I'm calling out your bluff!" But which one? Those are the only things this guy says. I envelop my entire body in flames and charge straight at him with all I have. The sound of metal banging onto the floor follows, but when I look back, there's not a dent on the suit.

"Ohhh. Good shot. Great shot, actually. Reminds me of this one!" He launches a barrage of missiles at me. Pssh! As if those are going to hit. I easily avoid all of them.

"Buddy, I think your idea of a good shot is a little skewed."

"Is it, though?"

"Huh? …OW!" The mist of the missile residue created an opening for him to come up behind me and smack me with the brush.

"Now to see what this suit can really do!" Trumboozle violently waves the brush in his hand like a kindergartener and creates duplicates of the suit with the paint it produces. "Bing! Bing! Bong! Bong! Bing! That's great. Humongous. Big. Great."

It seems the suits perform the same actions he does. That's interesting…

All of the suits fire more missiles at me. I avoid them again, but, this time, I'm prepared for his predictable counterattack. He goes behind me again, but as he smacks the brush into the ground, he misses me.

"Hey, Boozle! Up here." In my raised hand, I have a meteor, created from the excess dust that the missiles left behind.

"You can try all you want, chosen son, but it won't penetrate my suit AT ALL."

"Oh, won't it?" I'd recognize that booming voice from a mile away. Azilez is back! And her brush is with her. That's good. I thought the scientists used it to make the metal one Trumboozle is using.

"Sorry it took so long. D tried collecting a bunch of metal sticks to pound the guards with." Griff enters behind Azilez.

"It would've been awesome! Why'd you stop me-ee-ee-ee?" D bounces in place, pouting.

"LET HIM HAVE IT, V!" Azilez hammers her right fist into her left palm.

"With pleasure." I throw the meteor down. BOOM! The suits skyrocket toward me. Since the shields couldn't tank the meteor, I grab Trumboozle out of his suit and drop him in front of Azilez, Griff, and D, who all have their arms crossed. Azilez's right lip is puckered out of annoyance, and her face is seething red. I fly beside D and rub his head. He looks up and smiles. We then go out of our extreme forms and look right into Trumboozle's eyes.

"Don't worry. Don't worry. I know what you're thinking."

"You better. 'CAUSE YOUR LIFE DEPENDS ON IT." Azilez aims her brush at Trumboozle.

"Easy! Easy!" Griff forces her arm down.

"Hmph!"

"You could, at the very least, not deport us."

"Why should I do that? You've brought nothing but destruction. Just look around." I look at the destroyed lab room, expressionless. I don't want to show any signs of weakness here.

"And why is this room like this, you think?"

"Because you destroyed it with a meteor! Hello? Do I have to point out the obvious truth all the time? God, my job is just so hard sometimes–"

"OPEN YOUR EYES, FOR ONCE, YOU IDIOT!" Azilez can't contain her frustration. She grabs Trumboozle by his suit collar. It feels like her evil form is surfacing. I mentally prepare myself to stop her if she tries anything dicey. Though I can't really blame her. Trumboozle not only abused her power, but also made a cyborg so people don't ask what happened to the real Azilez. "YOUR INCOMPETENCE IS SO UNEBE-LIEVABLY BLIND THAT IT CAN'T COMPREHEND ANYTHING PAST WHAT IT ALREADY KNOWS. WHICH, BY THE WAY, IS NOT MUCH. SERIOUSLY! CHOSEN SON? WHERE DID YOU HEAR THAT? CAUSED

NOTHING BUT DESTRUCTION… HAVE YOU FOLLOWED WORLD NEWS AT ALL? WE SAVED THE WORLD TWICE. Well, I saved it once, but POINT IS, WE'VE DONE NOTHING TO DESERVE ALL THIS, AND I FEEL LIKE THE BARE MINIMUM YOU CAN DO IS PRETEND NONE OF THIS EVER HAPPENED. GOT IT?"

"Hmm…" Seriously? He's thinking about that? Even in the face of Azilez's punishment? She's right; he actually knows nothing of the world around him, even when it's right in front of him. "Oh! I see what's going on here." He stands up and dusts off his suit. Not like it matters because it's tattered to the point where it looks like he's wearing a cape. "Don't you worry. I'll have this settled by tomorrow. You'll see!"

"What are you going to say?" Griff is skeptical about Trumboozle's ability to settle things.

"There's no point if you know, right? That's why you'll just have to wait for me to say it. Good? Okay. Great. Bye bye, now." And just like that, he walks out of the room.

What just happened?

Chapter 4

Happy Birthday to Me!

Finally, back to relaxing. I can't stress this enough: I love not having to worry about anything, especially as of late. I mean, saving the galaxy twice can drain a guy, you know? I realize I won't be this relaxed forever, as the Unbound Evil will show up again, but, for now, I'll just enjoy the relaxation I have.

"Zzzz... zzzz... zzzz..."

– Zzzz... zzzz... zzzz.... Even the Dark Spirit is tired. And It has the literal power of God and the Devil flowing through It.

During my deep sleep, I have a dream. It's nothing too special, just me lying down on a patch of thin grass in a vast, green farmland. I'm looking up at the rolling clouds, comparing them to things I've seen throughout my now-14-year life.

Hmm... that one looks like the Sphinx in Egypt.

And that one looks like Transylvania's castle.

And that one looks like... it's coming right at me!

"Ooof! What the–"

"HAPPY BIRTHDAY, V!" Azilez bounces on my bed, forcing me off. THUD. I land, face first, on the wooden floor.

"*Yaaaawwwnn*... thanks, Azilez."

"You don't sound too excited about your birthday."

"Give me a sec. I just woke up..."

Just as I gather myself, Griff tackles me back onto my bed. He gives me a noogie as if he's my second older brother or something. Though, with what we've been through, he might as well be.

"Aw, yeah! Happy birthday, V." Griff releases me from his head-lock.

I shake my head to fix my hair and reorient my focus, again. I look once to the left and once to the right. "No one else is jumping on me today, right?"

"Nooooo promises." Azilez gets off my bed. She's wearing a casual pink-and-white dress, and her brush is in her right hand.

"So, V," Griff starts, "where'll we be going today?" He's wearing gray sweats and jacket, like a lounging cross-country runner.

"Um… I sort of forgot to plan this out, but the more I think about it, the more I realize that I didn't have to. Let's go out and explore the city as much as we can till the sun goes down!"

"W-w-w-w-w-wait! Pleeeease!" D bursts through the door to my room, wearing a buttoned floral top and cargo pants.

"Don't worry. We won't forget you, Z, and Vizor. Speaking of whom, where is he?" Griff asks.

"Still asleep, I think. Not a peep from his room."

"Ohhhh! I can't wait to wake him up." Azilez heads toward the door.

"Sorry. Not today." Z walks in, causing Azilez to bump her head on the door and fall over.

"What? How could you not come to V's birthday outing!" D puts his fists against his hips.

"No, no, D." Z chuckles at the misunderstanding. "That's not what I meant. *Of course* I'm coming." He puts no effort into his attire. He's been wearing his golf-tournament clothes for two days straight. Z's been busy golfing, though, so I won't say anything.

"UGH! Did you ever think to change, Z? You smell like a dumpster fire." Guess I didn't have to say anything after all. Azilez did it for me. Excellent.

"Strange way of saying 'Apologize for hitting me with the door.' Oh, by the way, sorry for hitting you with the door."

"That is NOT what I was–"

"Anyway," Z realizes this is going nowhere and veers back to his point, "what I was referring to when I walked in was that Vizor's sick."

"Oh." D whistles to try and ignore his own outburst.

"What's wrong with him, Z?" I ask.

"Well, it's hard to say because he's an alien 'n all, but he was cold. Like, really cold. Come see for yourself." Intrigued, we all go one story down the tree house into Z and Vizor's room. "Not sure how this happened. He seemed fine when I walked in here last night, but I woke up, mentioned V's birthday, and he literally froze."

"Ch-ch-ch-ch-ch-ch..." His teeth are chattering. His face also looks sky-blue. "S-s-s-sorry. I-I-I won't be-e-e-e-e comi-i-i-ing today."

"Ohh, you poor thing. Hang on, let me get an oral thermometer." Azilez rushes down to the kitchen. She scrambles through the utilities drawer until she finds a sticky thermometer. After thoroughly cleaning it with alcohol, she comes back up. "Here, let's take your temperature. Open wide." Vizor barely musters the strength to open his mouth. Azilez manages to get the thermometer under his tongue, though. ... Beep... beep... beep. After looking at the temperature, Azilez's jaw hits the floor. "S-s-s-s-SIXTY-TWO DEGRESS FARENHEIT?"

"Wait. What? That can't be right." Griff crosses his arms. He goes to Vizor's forehead to see for himself. After just getting close to Vizor, he feels how cold he is. "Never mind. I believe you. How is that possible?"

"Well, his race is the opposite of humans, right?" Z is actually thinking, for once. "If our heads heat up, then the opposite would be to cool down, right?"

"I guess. But *this* much? The human head only goes up by about two degrees."

"Z is r-r-right, V." Vizor cuddles his blanket more. "Back on T-T-T-T-T-Treah, we call this a f-f-f-freezer." Oh, haha. Very clever, Omoh sapiens. Freezer, instead of a fever.

– *Dark Spirit, do Your thing. ...Dark Spirit?*

It's still asleep? After all of that? Wow. Impressive.

– *Dark Spirit. Wakey, wakey!*

– *AH! What? Where? When? Oh. It's only you, V. I thought I was in danger.*

– Sorry to startle You.

– No, no, what did you require?

– Vizor's got a freezer. Can You go through him and fix it?

Oh...

That didn't sound very confident.

– Believe it or not, there are two things that I am not equipped to fix: freezers and fevers, since they are brought about by magical imbalances in the body. Sorry. I cannot do anything.

– Seriously? What about my evil form?

– Negative. Don't even think about it, normal V. My limitations are the same as the Dark Spirit's.

"S-s-s-sorry, everyone, but b-b-b-birthdays give me the chills." Vizor slouches deeper into his bed.

"How so?" Griff places his right index-finger square on his forehead.

"W-w-w-w-ell, o-o-o–"

"Hold on. You'll never be able to tell a story with all that chattering." I channel some heat from my extreme form to my left palm and grab Vizor's shoulder.

"Ahhh... t-thanks. Okay." Vizor takes a deep breath. "Back on Treah, I tried having a birthday once. Little did I know it was against Omoh sapien custom to celebrate a birthday. It is seen as an act of kindness."

"How is that a bad thing?" Azilez is quick to forget.

"Remember what I was saying about opposites, Azilez?" Z smirks as if his head contains all the knowledge in the world. "Anything here is opposite in Vizor's world."

"Right..." She puts her head down.

"Needless to say," Vizor continues, "it didn't end so well for me. I was nearly banished from Treah for trying. Even hearing the word 'birthday' gives me chills."

"I see. Well, if that's the case, you don't have to come. You've done a lot this past month, trying to adapt to Earth life and all. Why don't you just relax until we get back?"

"That sounds lovely. Thanks for understanding, V."

"No problem."

I wave, and the rest of us head out.

We first go to Pier 39, one of the busiest tourist spots in San Francisco... Or at least it would be if it were a weekend. It's practically empty right now. We start off on the lower level, eating copious amounts of clam chowder in bread bowls, pizza, burgers, fries, and chicken tenders.

Next, we head to the second story of the pier to find a bunch of tiny stores that sell all sorts of San Francisco-related merchandise. There, Azilez buys me a black Alcatraz T-shirt, Griff finds a gaming store and buys me a new *Sonic the Hedgehog* video game, and D and Z both pitch in to buy me three one-pound Hershey's chocolate bars.

After that, we stroll to the Exploratorium, a wonderland of science. It contains all sorts of neat do-it-yourself experiments. To give you an idea of how many: I've lived in San Francisco my entire life, and still haven't done all of them. New ones are constantly being added, like that dissection lounge. Except that one's not do-it-yourself. Imagine if it were, though. I could see the spilled guts and blade cuts from here.

Anyway, we end up staying there for about three hours, shocking ourselves, wearing prism glasses to play impossible basketball, creating floating illusions, talking to each other from hundreds of feet away using our normal voices, lifting the color out of our clothes and skin with gray-lit rooms (Azilez nearly fainted when she walked through the room and noticed there was no color anywhere), and making all sorts of funny scenes with the giant, distorted mirror.

Finally, we head back home to join our parents for the party's dinner and dessert. This is Azilez's section of the party; she handles everything in terms of food. And I wouldn't have it any other way. She is the best cook I know.

"Okay! Everyone ready?" Azilez claps her hands. She has her "Kiss the Chef!" apron on.

"Yeah!"

"Excellent! Griff, help me out."

"Okay."

My two best friends hustle and bustle in the kitchen. The main dish seems to be a chicken risotto with lemon zest. Let's see what she threw in with the chicken. There's rice. I like that. But... oh. Oregano, parsley, thyme, and onions. Eh. I'll tough it out. After all, she made all of this for my party.

"Calm down, V! I see that distaste in your eyes. Do you think I would make you a chicken like this?"

"You definitely got me." I'm a plain eater. The fewer ingredients in my food, the better. Azilez knows that, and she did this all to mess with me. Classic. "So, what did you make for me?"

"Glad you asked! Griff?"

"Here you go, V." My mouth waters at the sight of a salt-and-pepper fillet steak. "Hold on. That's not all."

"Oh, really?" I raise an eyebrow.

Griff heads back into the kitchen and comes out with a giant mac 'n cheese casserole. And when I say casserole, I mean literally just mac 'n cheese, with Ritz crackers crumbled on top.

"Dig in, everyone!" Azilez takes her apron off and sits next to her mom and Griff. Silence reigns throughout the dinner – which isn't a bad thing; it's the mark of a master chef because everyone is enjoying the food too much to talk.

BUUUUURRRPP.

"Ahh... satisfying as always, Azilez. Thanks a million."

"Not a problem at all! But now for the fun part."

"What's that?"

"Birthday speeches!"

Oh, God. I didn't prepare at all! I really wasn't ready for my birthday today, it seems. Well, everything's been going great today, and it's all been on the fly. So there shouldn't be a problem with doing the same thing for this. Besides, the birthday boy or girl always goes last. I have some time to think.

"My turn!"

Whoa, wait a second. Everyone has delivered speeches already – except for Azilez and Griff?

"Okay." Griff stands from his seat. "What can I say? Fourteen years. It's been a ride already, but it seems like only yesterday we met, V." I smile. I think I know where this is headed. "In fact, I don't think we've made the story of how we met public, have we, V?"

"No, we haven't, Griff. Feel free to tell it in all its glory!"

"All right, then. It was a muggy fall day, and we were both in pre-school. One recess, I see this kid with a fluffy, brown Afro playing with toy boats in a small container, with fresh water next to the pool."

"Why didn't V just play in the pool?" Griff's dad asks.

"That pool was filled with green swamp water. No one in the school maintained it. So when a preschooler wanted to play with water, he or she would just play with the container next to the pool. So, when I saw this, I went up to him and tried yanking the red toy boat out of his hands so I could play with it. He didn't want to let go, so we dove into a tug of war. After a few minutes of that, I dropped the toy boat, went up to him, grabbed him by the hair, and dunked his head in the pool."

"Let me intrude here for a second, Griff," I cut in. "At that moment, I decided, I'm not sure why, that I was interested in being friends with this person. Okay. I'm done. Continue, Griff."

He nods. "So after he catches his breath, he marches at me and undoes my Velcro vest, because, for some reason, he knew I hated wearing it. After that, we hugged and went back inside the classroom together, arm in arm. From that day forward, we swapped our pillows during naptime, as a sign of our friendship. I took his SpongeBob pillow, and he took my Cars one. And that's it."

The small group in the room claps, and Griff sits back down.

"I actually just noticed something," Kal, my dad, says. "Based on the way you described the story, it seems like you two didn't say a word to each other."

"That's because we didn't."

My dad's eyes pop.

"How did you do all of that without saying a word to each other?"

"Good question. Ask our three-year-old minds. Hahaha… In all seriousness, though, I can't really remember the exact reason, but I think it just goes to show how I knew that this guy right here would be my best friend. Happy birthday, V." Griff raises his glass of apple juice. The rest of the table raise their drinks and take sips. He sits back down.

"Okay, then. Azilez? Are you ready?"

"Absolutely! This won't take as long as Griff's." She stands up, sticking her tongue out at Griff. He replies with an "L" on his forehead. "So, this speech actually applies to both V and Griff. I haven't known you guys all my life, but I can say, without a doubt, that you two are the kindest, purest souls I've met. This is no origin story, but I think what happened during my 11th birthday best exemplifies what I mean." She retrieves her brush from under her chair. "This brush, the symbol of my strength now, was almost not given to me." Griff's parents and mine mumble among themselves. "My 11th birthday was almost cut short because one of my 'friends' destroyed my backyard right when she got there. She left the party, laughing maniacally. When everyone arrived at my party, they saw my crying face and simply left, except for two people: V and Griff. They stayed in my backyard all day, helping me clean up the damage. Then they gave me my presents. Griff gave me a canvas board set, and V gave me an art set, which included this brush. It was a joint gift, and I still use both items to this day. Thank you, both of you, and happy 14th, V!"

She sits down, raises her glass of water, and everyone drinks with her.

"Okay. I guess that leaves me, then." I stand from my seat at the head of the table. "Listen, everyone. I'm really thankful for what you've given me throughout my life. I don't think words can exactly describe what I feel right now, but just know that everyone in this room is near and dear to my heart. In fact, there are two people not in this room right now who are also near and dear to me, and whom I'd like to recognize: Vizor, because he has a freezer, as all of you know; and Rodger, who could not be here today because he is busy with his new military job. There is no one story that encompasses all of you together, so I cannot give a story like Griff and Azilez did. Just know that these past 14 years, and especially these two adventures we partook in, are the only story that can come close to describing my state of mind right now. Thanks to everyone in this room. My life would not be what it is without all of you. Cheers!" I lift my glass of grape juice high up, and a little liquid sloshes out. Everyone cheers with me as we take our final sip of the day.

After dessert, Griff bangs his velvet-covered fork against his glass of milk.

"Hold on, everyone. There's still one more thing left to do!"

"Really? I thought it was done by now." Even Azilez is lost.

"I prepared this last part without any of you knowing. It was done at the last second. And I couldn't do it without Rodger's help. So, V, this is Rodger's and my gift to you. Come outside, everyone." Outside? I like the sound of that. That means this gift is huge, whatever it is. Most of the fog from the day has cleared out, a rarity in San Francisco, but little did I know that this would result in the perfect conditions for the gift Griff was about to reveal. He takes out a walkie-talkie from his right pocket. "Okay, guys! Let it rip!"

He was talking to several fire trucks scattered throughout San Francisco. In a flash, fireworks fill the skies. Several different patterns are made, from SpongeBob to Sonic the Hedgehog, and to Knuckles the Echidna, the five Solar Prophecies, King Tut, racecars, past Azilez artworks, and the grand finale, a burst of letters that spell out "Happy Birthday, V."

I begin to cry. Thanks, Rodger and Griff. This is the best birthday ever.

Chapter 5

One-man Army from Beyond
- RODGER -

This new job is pretty easy.

Military threats nowadays are nonexistent, thanks to Griff, V, Azilez, Z, D, and Vizor. Their powers essentially keep the rest of the world in check, so all I have to do is train the new soldiers. After all, that's a commander's secondary duty.

"Move it, boys! You're fallin' behind. Let's go, go, go!" It's obstacle-course day on this fine, sunny day on the outskirts of San Francisco, and that means I get to see who's in shape and who's not. Based on the results, I'll know whom to train more in next week's boot camp.

Or at least that's what would've happened.

BRRRRRRR! BRRRRRR! BRRRRRR!

"General Rodger!" My transmission radio turns on. It's my boss, Trumboozle. "We need you and the air force in space, now."

"But I command the army, not the air force…"

"And that's an order!" It's not like I can say anything. He IS my boss, even though I don't think he realizes that there are five distinct military branches, namely the army, the navy, the air force, the coast guard, and the marines. Regardless, I have a job to do!

"Yes, Sir! … Hold on."

"What is it?"

"Did you say you need the air force and me in space?"

"Yes, is there a big problem with that?"

"May I ask why we're going into space?"

"A small, human-shaped thing is coming at Earth fast. Really fast. Humongously fast. We need you and the army to stop it."

I don't think humongously is a word… Also, didn't you say air force? It's fine. I'll just take my boys to avoid confusion. "Yes, Sir!"

"Good. Great. Be at the Florida NASA base in seven hours. The air force will escort you."

"So… which group of men am I fighting with?"

"The army."

I give up. This guy is impossible. I'll just figure it out when I get there.

"Boys! We're headed to Florida. It's an emergency situation. This is not a drill! Repeat! This is not a drill!"

"General Rodger. Here is your vessel." One of the aerospace engineers opens up the cockpit of a sleek, white fighter rocket with the blue NASA logo emblazoned on the vertical stabilizer.

"Thank you. Boys! Get to your assigned stations. After we take off, stay behind me. Further action will be communicated via our radios. Clear?"

"Yes, sir!" They salute and disperse.

"So, what does this threat look like?" I turn around and stare at the engineer who opened my rocket.

"We're not sure. It appears to be using camouflage. But it is definitely a human-shaped projectile. That is certain."

"Okay. Thank you."

"You're welcome."

I hop in my rocket, close the cockpit, and lift off from the launch base. The boys follow. Within minutes, we're outside the Earth's atmosphere.

"Ah… a sense of relaxation comes over me when I see the stars from here. Reminds me of the first time V, Griff, and I thwarted the Unbound Evil. Those were the days."

"General! We have a visual on the projectile. It appears to be a living being. Stay on guard." The computer screen to my right reveals a hooded figure. All I can see is the mouth, but that looks like a human chin to me. Why would a human be in space by him or herself?

"Be ready to fire, but do NOT shoot unless I give the order! Clear?"

"Yes, Sir!" When our ships approach the figure, it stops. "Boys! Stop!" I open my cockpit and attempt to communicate. "Hello. I am Rodger. Who are you?" I know it's mundane, but I do not want to alarm him or her.

"Nexus…" Okay, so it's a male, for sure. He has a decently deep voice.

"What? Your name is Nexus?"

"Give me Nexus, and I'll leave in peace."

"Who is Nexus? And who are you?"

"Who I am is not important. I only want my son back."

"Your son is Nexus? And he's on Earth? How do you know?" Before I could even react, he grabs me by my shirt collar and lifts me high. My boys want to shoot.

"DO NOT! DO. NOT. SHOOT! Sorry, but I don't know anything about someone named Nexus."

"Lies! You are a part of the organization that took him from me. Where is he? Tell me, or I'll throw you into deep space!" Oh, no! He really means it.

"Look. Let's talk this out. What does your son look like?"

"Long, white hair. Unforgiving, gold eyes, with a tyrant's expression."

That's pretty vivid. But that doesn't even sound human.

"I don't know where your son is. Honest. And what organization are you talking about? Who took your son from you?"

"The US government. Ten years ago." He throws me back into my cockpit with such force that the cockpit almost closes from the recoil. "Here." A small flash drive lands in the cup holder next to me.

"What is this?" I ask.

"Coordinates. For the Space Garden. Ask about the first human expedition to Mars."

"First expedition to Mars? That hasn't happened yet!"

"Or has it?" He turns around as if he's about to fly.

"Huh?" And there he goes. "Boys! Back to Earth. The threat is dealt with." At least I think it has been.

Chapter 6

The Breath of New Adventure

Ah... this is nice. Sitting on the couch, with a bag of cheddar sour-cream potato chips, watching SpongeBob with my best friends, two brothers, and newfound alien friend.

"None of you wetheads would last a minute on my turf," Sandy says.

"Do we have to wear pickle jars?" Squidward asks.

"HAHAHAHA!" All of us start cracking up.

"That might be Squidward's funniest beeline in the whole show!" D wipes a tear from his eye.

We all look back at the TV and are horrified to see that the channel has changed. D starts crying again, but this time it's not out of joy.

"WHO HAS THE REMOTE?" Azilez jumps from her seat, puckering the right side of her lips. We all look around. Vizor shakes his head. Griff shrugs. I wag my finger.

"Dearie, it was me." Candice shows herself from the kitchen.

"Why? Why would you do something so cruel?" D continues to cry.

"Easy, easy, now." Z pats his head.

"Remember? Trumboozle said he'd resolve the deportation issue with you guys. That interview is today, right now!"

"Ugh!" Azilez flings herself onto the couch and mumbles. "Might as well watch."

Candice raises the volume.

"Trumboozle! Over here! Over here!" The reporters begin clamoring like toddlers that eye a basket of cookies they can't reach.

"Yes, Miss. You." Trumboozle points and squints more as he plasters a smile on his face.

The female reporter stands from her seat. "Mr. President, you said a week ago that the super-powered kids from San Francisco were a menace to the world around them, and that they have done nothing to protect our home. Now, you stand here, attesting to the opposite. What created this change of heart?"

"Well, you see. It went like this." He lifts both his index fingers as if he's a maestro. "I wanted to see these guys for myself and see if they were really bad or not. And after having a nice lunch and a beautiful piece chocolate cake with all of them, I can safely say that they pose no threat at all. Their powers couldn't dent a fly even if they tried, believe me. Don't worry, I have it all under control."

"Good to hear. Thank you, Mr. President."

"Next question."

"THAT'S NOT WHAT HAPPENED AT ALL!"

"Azilez, I understand you're frustrated, but can we just listen to the… huh?" Candice looks over at Azilez's seat and finds that she's not there.

"Hold on. I think her voice came from the TV, Candice. Look!" I snag the remote from her and pause the interview. "Right there. She's sitting down, right in front of Trumboozle!"

"How did she get there so quickly?" Vizor asks.

"Trust me, if there's anything we've learned from her, it's that when she hates something, she despises it with all her being."

"That doesn't answer my question at all." Vizor slouches.

"Yeah, I don't know how she did it either," Griff replies.

"I guess that makes two of us, then."

"Make that three," I add.

"Four."

"Five."

"Six." Candice doesn't even know how Azilez practically teleported.

"FINALLY! HE'S DEALT WITH." Azilez knocks the door off its

hinges, snapping it in half.

"HOW DID YOU DO THAT?" Candice asks.

"DO WHAT?"

"TELEPORT FROM HERE TO THE WHITE HOUSE."

Azilez's demeanor makes a complete 180. She smiles, snaps her fingers, winks, and says, "Don't worry about it. Teehee."

"What'd you say to him?" Vizor is curious.

"Un-pause the TV. You'll see."

"Okay, then." Vizor rips the remote out of my hands and finds the pause button.

"THIS MAN IS A CRIMINAL," Azilez continues on TV. "HE FORCEFULLY CAPTURED ME AND USED ME AS A POWER SOURCE FOR A MECHANICAL SUIT. HE THEN TRIED USING SAID SUIT TO KILL MY FRIENDS."

The reporters mumble amongst themselves, while Trumboozle tries to call for the security that Azilez knocked out.

"Trumboozle, is this true?" One of the male reporters asks, holding out his phone to record Trumboozle's answer.

"Of course not! This girl is just making up stories. If there's fake news anywhere in this country, it's with her!"

"THEN HOW DO YOU EXPLAIN THESE?" Azilez reaches into her back pocket and takes out three photographs. One is of the suit, the second is of Trumboozle attacking me, and the last one is of Azilez in the suit-testing facility, before we arrived to save her.

"Those could've been made anywhere. You're an artist, aren't you? You could've easily fabricated those."

"Unlikely." Bessie walks into the room. "I'm an eyewitness that saw your men attack and capture Azilez in the Ghirardelli store I work at."

The reporters gasp and turn to Trumboozle to see him react. "That means nothing. You two are friends, right? More fake news!"

"Enough, Trumboozle." One of the scientists from the abandoned factory walks through the already-open press-conference doors. "Those photos are real. They're from the underground facility's cameras.

I can attest to this fact."

"It means nothing. You're fired!"

"If he's fired, you'll have to fire me too." Another scientist walks into the buzzing chaos.

"And me."

"And me."

"Me too!"

"Me three!"

"You're not firing him."

Eventually, a crew of about 30 scientists walks into the room.

"Hmm… I can just fire all of you." Trumboozle puts his hands up and shrugs.

"Boooooo!" The entire room goes nuts.

"Impeach him! Throw him in jail," one of the reporters in the back yells.

"Trumboozle? More like Trum'beelze'le!" the reporter that asked the first question screams.

"Trumb is dumb!" a third cries out.

After the uproar dies down a little, the FBI runs in and handcuffs Trumboozle, leading him off the podium, into a police car, and to a detention center. Good riddance.

"You did all of that this quickly?"

"He deserved it. You don't mess with me and get away with it!"

This is true. Azilez is scary when she's angry.

"Anyway," Azilez takes out her brush and materializes some chicken-noodle soup, "here, Vizor. You'll need it to get better."

"Actually, I don't need it. The red-velvet cake you made did away with my freezer."

"How can cake…? Oh, wait! Opposites. Duh! Unhealthy food cures you. Well, that's good to hear. Guess I'll have the soup then."

"Can we watch SpongeBob now?" D asks, reaching for the remote in Vizor's hand.

"Sure, D," Vizor says, and changes the channel for him. We all sit back down on the couch, and Candice disappears into the kitchen again.

"Wait! Let me fix the door first." Azilez takes out her brush and conjures up a rainbow paste. She flicks it onto the two door pieces, which brings them back together. Using her brush like a wand, she creates another rainbow to fit the door back into place. "Okay. NOW let's watch." She jumps back into her seat and wiggles around to get comfortable.

"Oops. I think I finished the bag of chips." My lips are orange from the cheddar bits.

"Was it full?"

"No." Yeah, it was totally full.

– *Nice, V,* Vizor communicates telepathically.

– *Not a word about this to my parents, got it?*

– *Oh, sure. No problem.*

– *I see your fingers crossed behind your back.*

– *Curses! Foiled again.*

– *Hahahaha!* We both laugh in our minds.

Our telepathic communication is interrupted by a knock at the door. It's probably my dad, Kal, although it's rather early for him to come from work. It's only 3 o'clock.

"Who is it?"

"Rodger! General Rodger. Open up, guys." Out of pure excitement, Griff and I nearly leap from the couch to the door.

"Hey! It is you." I give him a hug. Griff follows. He's still in uniform. I guess he just got off work.

"How are you guys?"

"Awesome! Couldn't be more relaxed right now."

"That's good to hear. By the way, happy birthday, V." Rodger reaches into his pocket and takes out a half-crushed gift. I tear it open, and it contains a video-game controller.

"Thanks, Rodger. For this, for the fireworks, and everything in between." I hug him again.

"Not a problem at all. I'm not in my military outfit just for kicks, though. There's something really serious I need to talk to you guys about."

"What is it?" Griff asks.

"It has something to do with my latest mission. And since you're all working for us now, it involves you too. Come with me."

We follow Rodger outside, down the ladder to the base of the front porch. Some of his men are waiting on the front lawn, with a private military aircraft to escort us to DC's Capitol Building. We all hop in.

"So, how's your new job been, Rodger?" Griff asks.

"Honestly, pretty uneventful. I mainly just train my boys, day by day. The world is largely at peace because of all of you. I'm very thankful for that."

"We take cash or credit," Azilez jokes around.

"Heh. Anyway, back to the matter at hand. While I did say that the world is safe, the galaxy might not be."

"Is it the Unbound Evil again?" I roll my eyes.

"Actually, no." This is different. "While on my latest defense mission, I was sent into outer space to prevent a fast-moving obstacle from impacting Earth. It turns out that obstacle was a human, and it gave me this flash drive."

"What did it want? And what was on the flash drive?" Z asks.

"I'm not 100% sure yet, but he said that there were coordinates in there for the Space Garden. Also, he wanted his son back because the government took him ten years ago."

"What is the son's name?" D asks.

"Nexus. Do any of you know someone with that name?" We mumble amongst ourselves for a little while, but come up with nothing. "Okay, then. No big deal. We'll appease him some other way."

"Sir, we're approaching the target destination." One of Rodger's men comes out and salutes him.

"At ease. Excellent. We'll be ready."

The soldier walks back into the cockpit and smoothly lands the plane next to the Capitol Building.

Rodger bursts into a room where five scientists are waiting. Inside, it's dimly lit, incredibly spacious, and smells like the scientists just got off a snack break because their breath smells like veggies and salad.

"Good evening, General Rodger. Do you have the device for me to inspect?"

"Right here, Head Scientist Jaclyn."

"Excellent. One moment, please, while I map out the Milky Way." Jaclyn punches in some numbers into a massive keyboard in front of her, and a projector shoots out a 3D map of the entire Milky Way. The celestial disc is astoundingly detailed, depicting every star and sector within the galaxy. "Now allow me to plug in this flash drive here. This is where the Space Garden is."

A red dot flashes in the center of the galaxy.

"Can you get a close-up picture of what the place looks like?" Rodger asks.

"Negative. The Milky Way's core gives off too much light for any known camera to be able to focus on it."

"That's fine. There can only be so many places near a black hole," Vizor says.

"I actually had a question too, Jaclyn. Was there ever a human expedition to Mars? No, right?"

"… Who told you about that?" Uh oh. I don't like that pause.

"The mystery man that gave me the flash drive."

"This is bad. Come with me, now." The urgency in her voice prompts all of us, including the other scientists, to follow closely. "Apologies. Not you four. I was referring to our guests. This is a matter of top-secret information. Stay here." The scientists stay behind, and we follow Jaclyn into a nearby elevator. She swipes her government ID into the card reader, does a retina scan and fingerprint test, then pushes the bottommost button in the elevator. "Stay close. Do not wander off."

When the elevator door opens, we see only darkness. Jaclyn flips a light switch, and several bulbs beam brightly. The light reveals several shelves filled with giant, dusty files. She continues walking. We continue to follow. There's an eerie feeling in here. No sound is coming from anywhere – except for our footsteps, thanks to the thick concrete walls.

"Where… where are we?" D's apprehension makes him shiver.

"An archive of US government operations. All of them, even the ones the public does not know about." That doesn't make D feel any better. It's even scaring me a little bit. What could've happened ten years ago on Mars that was kept from the public? Jaclyn stops at a shelf in the corner. She takes one big puff and blows away all the dust in the area. It gets in my hair. I shake my head to get it all off. "Let me see... here. This is the file for the KFIJ-5711 project. Code name: Project Mutant." Jaclyn pulls out the smallest file in the shelf.

"Mutant? Huh..." Griff places his right index finger on his forehead.

"This was the first human expedition to Mars... Or at least that's its cover for its true purpose." D continues to shiver. Z holds him. "Ten years ago, there was a contest that would allow 5,000 people to go to Mars to see if life could be sustained there. But, as I just stated, that was not the true purpose of the project. It was an attempt to see if the US government could create super humans, endowed with abilities much like the ones you all have right now. However, shortly after the launch of the project, communications were lost, and the rocket that contained all of the people vanished. Our satellites could not find any remains of the rocket or the people onboard. None of them were ever heard from again. At least until now."

"You're talking about that mystery person?" Rodger just wants to verify.

"Precisely. Seeing as there were no other failed attempts at a space mission outside of the Earth's atmosphere, it must be so. If you're certain that the thing you saw in outer space was a human, then yes, that person is likely from that 'failed' project."

"Why'd you say 'failed' like that?" Azilez asks.

"Because if a person from this mission survived, that means that the mission actually had a chance to succeed. And there may be an army of super mutants out in space that we don't know about."

"And you're concerned that they'll try and destroy the Earth for the way the government treated them?"

"Precisely."

"That doesn't make sense, though." Griff finally takes his finger off his forehead.

"Why do you hypothesize that?" Jaclyn asks.

"If the army really wanted to destroy the Earth, why would they send coordinates of where they are in the galaxy?"

"Hmm... excellent question, Griff." Jaclyn sounds pleased. "It seems there is more to this mystery man than meets the eye."

I begin to smile.

"What's up, V?" Griff looks my way.

"Well, if there's more than meets the eye, then I say we go investigate ourselves and see what's really going on at this Space Garden." Griff nods his head. "Ah... smell that, everyone?"

"What? The dust? Yeah, it's terrible." Z smirks.

"No. Not that. It's the smell of a new adventure!"

Chapter 7

The Space Garden

It feels good to put the ol' adventure gear back on. For me, that includes a red T-shirt with a big white "V" right in the middle, and black sweats.

"You guys ready? C'mon! I've been waiting for a half hour now," I holler.

"We're all ready, V," Griff shouts back. "It's Azilez that's taking forever."

"I NEED to straighten my hair. It doesn't do that by itself, you know! Actually, wait a second. My paintbrush might be able to do it for me! ... There. All done." I waited a half hour for this?

Azilez, Griff, Vizor, Z, and D walk out of the tree house. Z walks off the entrance and face-plants the grass, D carefully climbs down the ladder because of his pickaxe, Azilez summons a rainbow board and hovers down, and Griff and Vizor just jump down.

Griff and Azilez are also wearing their iconic adventure gear. Griff's bright-orange shirt gleams in the morning sun and his gray pants and backpack contrast it perfectly. Azilez's tie-dye tank top clashes as much with her fingerless biker gloves and waist-cut leather jacket as with her emotions, and the jean shorts finish the look.

"So the Solar Prophecies are in there this time, right?" I recall the last adventure we had when the Devil just snatched the five talking miracle tablets, right under our noses.

"Positive." Griff zips open the biggest section of the backpack. Four of them are there. Of course, the Speed Prophecy is missing. "Speedy! Where are you?"

"S-sorry! I'm coming." Yeah, I know. They talk. Weirder things have happened, trust me. POW! It hits the left side of the entrance on its way out and flips onto the grass. It almost blends in, with it emitting slime-green light and all. "I was helping Azilez do her hair. But then she just waltzed out of the bathroom, and I couldn't find her."

"Don't worry about it. I'm here now, right?" She snaps her fingers.

"I guess so. All right, Griff. Throw me in!"

"Oh, dear..." the Prophecy of Wisdom murmurs.

"Gonna be one of those days again, isn't it?" I bet the Power Prophecy would roll its eyes if it had any.

"I haven't even said anything yet..."

"Correct, Speed Prophecy, but we all know you eventually will. You simply cannot help yourself," Wisdom replies.

"Aw! You guys know me so well." The Speed Prophecy dances in the bag.

"Hey, hold on." Griff scrambles through the bag. "The Shadow Prophecies aren't in here! Vizor, where'd you put them?"

"Guess." It seems like Vizor just remembered something because he has a silly grin on his face.

"In your hair? With your grappling hook? Because I'm sensing something coming from there," Griff replies.

"Close. Watch this!" Vizor detaches his blades from his hair. "Come on out." From the handles of the blades, black mist fills the surrounding air, and five floating black tablets form.

"Wow. They fit in your blades?" Z raises an eyebrow.

"As it turns out, yeah. They're quite compact and easy to carry. I barely even feel the extra weight."

"Mind if I put my clubs in there too?" Z asks.

"I don't think those'll fit..."

"All right. Enough chitchat. You guys ready?" I get everyone back on track. "Center of the Milky Way, here we come!" I hover above the ground, signaling I'm about to take off. Everyone does the same, and we launch into outer space.

We make it to the Space Garden with no problems. The blinding light shielding the center of the galaxy was more annoying than hindering, as we merely blasted through it, but then I realized the black hole is still there! I have to be ready to pull everyone out at once, just in case its gravitational pull catches us off–

"WOW! It's so pretty!" Azilez gushes over the abundance of cube-shaped, yellow flowers.

I got to give it to her, though: the light emanating from these flowers is nothing like the blinding mess from the shield of the galaxy's core. It looks and feels as though each flower has a compact sun inside. It's like the sun was a frog and gave birth to, say, 100,000 tadpoles.

As a matter of fact, there's more: thousands upon thousands of asteroids, some with homes on top, as well as a twisted, translucent yellow road connects them all. For the icing on the cake, a city-sized castle with ten watchtowers and three enormous spiraling bases.

"I guess this is why it's called the Space Garden. Every floating rock here has some flowers." Vizor looks around. "And look down there. The black hole! Why is it not sucking in any of the rocks?"

"Good question, bro!" Out of the blue, a bright-yellow-skinned, human-like figure flies off the biggest floating rock and greets us with a smile. He has a military-style toothbrush haircut that makes his hair go straight up, is wearing sandals and shades, and has a black tank top on. "Welcome to the Space Garden. Here, everything is… uh. Hold up. Sorry. I'm bad at this." His voice resembles that of a surfer boy straight out of Hawaii. He reaches for his pocket and takes out a notecard. "Eh-hem! Welcome to the Space Garden, the only place in the Milky Way that is powered by a black hole. Enjoy our abundance of Ophoozi flowers and complimentary tour, provided by me, King Veniss."

"A tour, huh?" Griff holds his finger to his forehead again, sounding awfully suspicious. Something's definitely got him on edge.

– *Griff? What was that? The king of this place offers us a tour, and you're indifferent?*

– *Agreed. Quite rude,* The Dark Spirit adds.

– *Don't you guys feel it?* Griff externalizes… internally. – *This king has no presence.*

    – No presence? What do you mean? I ask.

    – It's like… he has no soul. It's hard to explain, but there's nothing being emitted from his body. No spirit, no energy, nothing! It's weird.

    – Well, we're dealing with potential mutants here, Griff. The experiment the government performed on them could've taken away their sense of self. I brainstorm with him.

    – That's a good point, but I'll still keep a watchful eye. I've never felt this before.

    – Sounds good, buddy.

"So, do you guys wanna see stuff in the main castle? It's pretty much the only thing this place has, other than the flowers. Every other building you see is a house."

"Sure, why not?" D jubilantly accepts King Veniss. Everyone follows, except for Z. He materializes a golf set and starts playing off the flowers.

"So, what brings you dudes here?" Veniss turns around, hops, and bursts his legs with bright-yellow energy that allows him to hover.

"Whoa! How are you doing that?" I'm tempted to touch the yellow energy.

"Oh, this?" King Veniss points at his legs. "I'm not sure. As far as I know, I was born like this."

"Interesting…" I twirl my hair.

"I want to see the castle! I want to see the castle!" D jumps up and down.

"Chillax, dude. I'm opening the gate." With a hefty push, the towering ornate gate parts, and the foyer is revealed. Inside, a purple carpet covers the floor, and five glass chandeliers illuminate the room. Several hundred slightly yellow, noseless citizens are busy conversing. Many have wine glasses in their hands, filled with some tough, orange substance. We take a step back to take it all in. Azilez inspects the chandeliers more closely, studying their intricate designs, and D gazes at the potted plants filled with Ophoozi flowers. "So this is the place where anyone can go. It's like a place where business stuff happens and all that."

"Are you involved in business processes in any way?" Vizor asks the king.

"Nah. I don't do business. I'm more cerimeee… Wait, no. That's not right. Cerimaaaa… cerimmmm…"

"Ceremonial, Veniss. It's pronounced 'ceremonial.'" A royal figure with a massive, twisted staff descends some of the stairs that lead to the upper floors. She's wearing a blue dress, puffed up by the fur on the shoulders. Some of her straight, blond hair is rolled up on both sides of her head, and her commanding yellow eyes exhibit the force of a thousand soldiers. For some reason, though, her skin is pale like a human's. "Are you having trouble memorizing the one duty I have entrusted you with?" She crosses her arms, her expression unchanged.

– *There it is again, V! This queen also has no sense of self. I can't feel a thing.*

– *Is everyone else in the foyer like that? I ask.*

– *Everyone except us. …Oh.*

– *Told you. It's probably just because they're mutants.*

– *Ngh. It still bothers me.*

"Ah, don't worry 'bout it, sis. I'll have it down pat by next week." He flies up to her, and pats her on the back.

"It's been three months since I've asked you to memorize it, and you've come up empty. I doubt a week will change that." She pounds her staff on the ground. A bright light beams into the five chandeliers, catching Azilez off guard. The throng of citizens inside the foyer parts with military precision to make way for the queen. "At any rate, it appears you have brought guests. Excellent! We shall give them the proper greeting." Griff braces himself. For a few seconds, the chandeliers turn off, only to burst to life with erratic fireworks. They smack all the citizens up, down, and all around the foyer, like playing Ping-Pong with human-shaped balls. Despite that, the citizens begin cheering as if used to getting smacked in the face by fireworks. We try our best to avoid the incoming explosives. "Welcome, honored guests! I am Queen Neona, absolute monarch of the Space Garden."

Chapter 8

Castle Kusondela

Absolute monarch, huh? That's impressive, and she barely looks older than any of us. Maybe I should be studying royalty to be like her one day. I mean, this queen seems way better at her job than the king. I wonder how she became queen this young. That's probably a touchy subject though, as typically the queen's mother has to die for that to happen. Better not ask till the time's right... if it'll ever be right.

"Come along, everyone. I will give you a PROPER tour of Castle Kusondela." The queen glares at King Veniss. He just puts his hands behind his head as if he's on a hammock. "This way, please. Veniss, walk behind me. I'll teach you how to properly give tours of the castle again." She points her hand to where she came from. All of us follow her. "Be sure to follow only where I go. This castle has a peculiar... how should I put this... glitch."

"What do you mean by that?" Azilez asks, making sure her brush is still in her back pocket.

"It's one of the consequences of being powered by a black hole. You see, occasionally, there will appear a dark-blue-lit room in which there is nothing but a podium and a cassette tape. If you ever see this while in the castle, run back to the door through which you entered. Otherwise the black hole will consume you." "WHAT? That's a big glitch." Azilez's heart skips a beat.

"Do not worry, for I can sense when this will happen because of my uncanny ability to manipulate light at will."

"Wait. So that fireworks show when you greeted us wasn't the

44

staff's doing? That was you?" Griff asks.

"Yes." He shows approval and nods. "Now then, let me see..." She places her left hand on one of the diamond-shaped, carpeted doors. "This room is not glitched. Enter."

"She's so poised," Azilez whispers to Vizor.

"So it would seem." Vizor agrees, except he forgets to whisper.

"So it would seem... what?" Queen Neona slowly turns her head.

"Umm..." Vizor freezes from the chills Neona sends down his spine.

"Hahaha! Do not fret. I'm simply joking." Huh. I didn't expect that from her. Who knew a monarch so commanding could have a decent sense of humor too? "Come, please. I insist." She guides us with her hand once more.

Inside the almost opaque room, there seems to be a giant computer monitor with a few hundred smaller monitors surrounding it. At each small monitor, there is an employee wearing a bright-yellow jumpsuit and an orange biker helmet. The big computer screen shows what appears to be a radar map.

"What is this place?" I ask.

"Our military head. This is Star Security's headquarters. You may have noticed the lack of anything other than houses outside of the castle."

"Yeah, we did," I reply.

"Well, that is because everything in our society is run through this castle. The black hole powers the castle, and the castle powers the houses and the people within them. This proves to be an effective system because nothing in this universe can counteract a black hole. Not even light. It is the ultimate energy source."

"How advanced!" Vizor is suddenly fascinated with the potential technology in the room.

– Hold on, Vizor, Griff interrupts. – This is the military headquarters, right? They might know about Project Mutant, and I'd say right now is the best time to ask.

– Keen senses, Griff. Thanks. "Excuse me, Queen Neona?"

"What troubles you, err... what are your names? Forgive me for not asking." She bows.

"No trouble. My name is Vizor."

"I'm Azilez!"

"D. I love the flowers outside."

"Griff."

"V."

"Hey! Aren't you going to introduce us too, Griff?" The Speed Prophecy shakes Griff's backpack. Griff grabs the straps with both hands to make sure the backpack doesn't fly off his shoulders.

"My, my. What do we have here?" The queen tilts her head.

"Uh... nothing, nothing!" Griff quickly shakes his hands.

"Are you certain? I'm positive I heard a sound being emitted from your sack."

"All in your imagination!" Griff smiles. – *Wisdom! Tell Speedy to shut up! I don't want the queen knowing about you five.*

– *Why is that? I see no harm in it.*

– *Just do it, please. Sorry I snapped. I just sort of panicked.*

– *Very well.* The prophecies murmur amongst themselves.

"Oh, okay. Sorry," The Speed Prophecy actually whispers.

"All right, then. If there is nothing of interest in the sack, I shall introduce you to our commander. Rod! Front and center."

"Yes, Ma'am! Reporting for duty." Rod salutes the queen. He's wearing a uniform that's different from everyone else's. It consists of a dark-green military jacket, probably to stand out from the rest of the soldiers, a cap with a bright-yellow star in the middle, and black cargo pants. He also has extremely long, silver hair that goes out in ten different directions. Now that's a wild hairstyle, and that's coming from me.

"Calm." The queen raises her left hand. Rod slams his hand to his side.

"What is the command, Your Majesty?"

"Nothing of dire importance. Merely to introduce yourself to our guests."

"Right away, Ma'am! Hello, everyone. I am Commander Rod,

head of Star Security. Are you enjoying your tour of the castle so far?"

"Yes! Yes! Yes!" D jumps.

– *Okay. My powers are broken,* Griff concludes.

– *Why do you say that?* I telepathically ask.

– *You can very clearly see that this commander is in a good mood, right?*

– *Yeah.*

– *My powers are telling me that he has crippling depression.*

– *If I were you, I'd just ignore your powers here.*

– *Same.*

"So, commander. What do you generally protect your people from? I doubt you get many visitors, being this close to a black hole," Azilez asks.

"Excellent question, Miss. Our primary threat is our neighbors in the Phantom Pipeline."

"The Phantom Pipeline?" D asks.

"Yes. It is a world filled to the brim with Derpy-looking gray ghosts. Lately, many of them have been invading our territory, so it's my job to lead the fight to drive them away."

"Teehee. He said Derpy," Azilez chuckles.

"No, seriously. That's the most accurate description I can give those things. I have a picture of one. I can show you." He reaches into his jacket pocket and finds a crumpled photo. He straightens it out and blows on it to make it more visible. "They all look the same, by the way." Would you look at that? He's right. This ghost is a rounded trapezoid that has four droplet-like figures coming from the bottom of it. It kinda looks like snot that just won't fall out of a nose. It also just has two big white circles for eyes and no mouth.

"I think it looks cute." Azilez holds her brush in both hands.

"That's really the only thing you can say about it?" Vizor rolls his eyes.

"Where do they come from?" D asks.

"The Phantom Pipeline," Rod replies.

"Oh, no. I meant to say where is the way to the Phantom Pipeline? How do they get here?"

"Ah! Excellent question. If I knew, I'd be in their territory. That's actually what we're working on right now."

"So that's what the radar map is for?" I ask.

"Bingo, kid." Rod puts his hands on his hips. "Your Majesty, may I have your permission to return to my position immediately?"

"Permission granted, commander."

"Thank you, Your Majesty!" He salutes her once more and pants back to his post at the main computer.

"I believe you have seen and heard everything the headquarters has to offer. Shall we depart?"

"Please!" D tugs on her dress. The queen smiles in return. She taps D's wrist with her staff, signaling him to stop tugging.

"So where are we now?" I ask. It looks like some sort of factory. Hundred-foot-tall steel supporters erupt from the ground to the ceiling. The temperature in here is colder than the foyer and Star Security's headquarters. I eye some laborers in loose white suits who seem to be packaging that tough orange fluid I saw everyone drinking earlier.

"This is the Manufacturing Department," Queen Neona responds. "All items that my people require are made in this room."

"This factory doesn't seem too big, considering it makes everything for your people," Griff points out. "How much do your people need exactly?"

"Well," the queen adjusts her posture, "in terms of food, hardly anything. Syrusima is all they need to thrive."

"Seee-rooo-sym-uh?" Vizor tries pronouncing the word, syllable by syllable.

"Your people eat only one thing for their whole lives?" Azilez looks like she's seen a ghost. "I'd rather suffer purgatory!"

"Hahaha! You amuse me, Azilez." The queen lets out a child's laugh. "But in all seriousness, Syrusima contains all the nutritional value my people need. And it can be mass-produced. Not a soul in the Space Garden has gone hungry ever since my team came up with this concoction."

"We should tell the people back home about this. It'll solve world hunger!" Griff gets excited.

"I'm afraid not." Neona's face dips. "The ingredient for making it can only be found in the Ophoozi flower. These flowers can grow only here in the Space Garden, and their properties are due to a combination of the black hole powering Castle Kusondela and the meteorites they grow on. I'm sorry, but getting Syrusima to the humans on Earth would be an impossibility."

"Aw…" Griff's internal light bulb turns off.

The queen then shows us what other types of products they make in the Manufacturing Department, from furniture to clothes, and even houses that the people here live in. Then we reach the magnetic section.

"What are those?" I ask, pointing.

"Ah, yeah! Dude, check this out," Veniss finally speaks. He runs up to one of the scientists and snatches a U-shaped magnet. He flicks the switch on the arc of the magnet to turn it on. Everything in the room is pulled in by its magnetic pulse.

"Veniss! Turn it off, this instant!" Neona snaps at him.

"'K, geez, sis." He flicks the switch in the other direction, and we all stop. "You're no fun at all sometimes."

"That's because I actually know how to take my job seriously!" Neona barks. Veniss squints but doesn't stop smiling.

"What just happened?" D's eyes widen.

"That is our latest project. Infusing the properties of a black hole inside a magnet. Although the magnet cannot consume objects, it can attract anything to it."

"That'd be an amazing weapon in battle," Vizor points out. "Let all of your enemies come to one area, then drop this on them to ensure they can't move. Finally, annihilate all of them at once with a large explosive."

"It seems someone is well-versed in the field of battle." Neona smirks. "Yes, it can be used that way – though they are difficult to make. That is the only one we have created so far out of a few thousand attempts."

"What do you do with the ones that don't work?" D asks.

"Well, a few years ago, we collected all the defects in a pod and sent it to the Asteroid Belt of your solar system."

Wait a second. Magnets in the Asteroid Belt? I've heard that before! "I think your magnets may have formed sentient life forms, Your Majesty."

"What makes you think that, V?" She crosses her arms.

"About two months ago, while on an adventure, Griff and I stumbled upon a race of floating magnets in the Asteroid Belt on a small, magnetic planet called Zapzoid. Their planet was destroyed by artificial means, but the remains were taken to a site near San Francisco and built upon. It became its own city, called Zaptropolis."

"Good heavens! Are you certain they're magnets? And are you certain they are sentient?"

"Hundred-percent yes to both of those questions, Your Majesty."

"Then it seems I must send a team to investigate. Thank you for the information."

"My pleasure."

"Anyway, it is best we don't get too distracted from the tour. Come, there is more to see."

Next, we go through a door that leads us above a place that features the architecture of a theater, but the structure of a courthouse. It contains a shiny, wooden witness stand, a marble tile floor with a picture of the sun on it, two wooden attorney benches, and a protruding judge's chair. We can see that a trial is going on but can't hear anything because of a thick, glass dome in front of us.

"What you are seeing now is the work of the Absolute Court. This is where criminals, both domestic and foreign, are tried for the crimes they are accused of, as it is the only court in the Space Garden."

"What's going on in there now?" Vizor asks.

"I suppose it's… a foreign case. It seems the Phantom Pipeline is still a problem here. When you leave the castle today, I will have the king escort you to your quarters to ensure your safety."

"How nice of you. Thanks!" Azilez claps her hands together.

"Since the trial is currently in session, we cannot observe for long, so come. We wouldn't want to distract them, would we?"

"No, Miss!" D tries his best to sound official.

"And this is the end of the tour." Neona opens the final door. "These are my private quarters."

"How extravagant! How big are those Corinthian columns? What type of canvas is that painting of you made of? What is…" Azilez can't contain her questions.

"I see you like my choice in design, Azilez?" the queen detects.

"ABSOLUTELY! I could study this room for days."

"Calm down, tiger. We should let the queen get back to her business. She is a QUEEN after all." Griff holds Azilez's shoulder.

"Y'know? You're right. Bye, Your Majesty!"

"Please, call me Neona. No need for such formalities."

"Okay! Bye, Neona."

"Thanks for the tour. It was awesome!" D tugs her dress again.

"Not a problem, little D." She bends down and taps his forehead with her staff. D giggles and runs back to me. "Veniss!"

"'Sup?"

"Please escort our guests to their quarters." She reaches for her bedside drawer, takes out some sticky notes, tears one off, and clicks a pen open. She scribbles some directions, then thrusts the scrap of paper into Veniss' hands.

"You got it, sis."

"Excellent. Now, if you'd excuse me, I have some military matters to attend to."

Chapter 9
Ominous Otherworldly Menace

"'K, dudes. Here's your pad for now." Veniss opens the door to a house that has a couple of beds and a bathroom.

"Excellent. That's all we'll need. Thanks, Veniss." I pat him on the back.

"Don't worry 'bout it. Hope you like it here." He closes the door and flies back to Castle Kusondela.

"Well, this is cozy." Azilez plops onto one of the beds. She snuggles in one of the fluffy yellow blankets.

"I'll say. This toilet seat has a butt warmer!" Griff hollers from the bathroom.

"I'm tired. That was a lovely first day." I stretch my arms, then fall onto one of the other beds. My Afro sinks into the soft, white pillow. Ahhhh… one sheep… two sheep… three–

"FOUR!" A golf ball crashes through the only window in the house and collides with one of Vizor's hair blades, causing it to cut in half. Azilez panics and falls off her bed, tangled in her blanket.

"Z!" She storms to the door, but Z opens it right in her face, and she plummets.

"Guys? Did my ball come in here?" Z is holding a seven iron.

"Ugh…" Azilez holds her hand up.

"What happened to you?" Z smirks.

"I'm just gonna go back to bed…" Azilez doesn't even bother replying to Z. After picking herself up, she walks by the window and waves her brush. A rainbow envelops the window, and the broken glass is filled in.

"No hard feelings, right, Azilez?" Vizor helps Z find the two pieces of his ball. She reaches for her brush on the side-table drawer, points it at Z, and a rainbow hammer flies into his chest. "Ooof!" Z tumbles. As he collects himself, he eyes Azilez sticking her tongue out at him. She turns back over and falls asleep.

"Aha! Here's the second half, Z." Vizor picks up the perfectly cut half-sphere.

"Yeah, I think this is a signal to stop for the day." Z examines the two pieces. "Though it's loads of fun to play here. The lower gravity makes my ball go higher, which allows for a ton of new hole-design options."

"Did you see any trees?" D is curious.

"Nah. Just those Ophoozi flowers."

"You think if we ask the queen she'll let me plant some?" D's eyes light up.

"I don't see why not. C'mon, I'll go with you." Z pats D on the head.

"Okay!" D grabs his pickaxe and marches out the door.

"Hey, wait! I just got here." Z yanks his seven iron off the tile-carpet floor and rushes after him.

Now then, back to sleeping…

Okay! I feel refreshed and ready to go back to the castle. This time, I'll see what Project Mutant's impact was on this place.

I jump out of bed and head to grab a granola bar from Griff's backpack. Since everyone else is still asleep, I decide to go outside to eat. I want to take in the scenery – the shiny yellow road, the flowers, the different styles of homes, and most of all, the castle with the black hole under it!

Let's see, the granola bars should be in this side zipper…

"Psst! V, over here." The Solar Prophecy whispers from the big zipper.

"Do you guys want some fresh air?" I ask.

"Please!"

"We're also rather concerned with something." The Wisdom Prophecy speaks up.

"Oh, okay. Let's go outside and talk." I unzip the big zipper, and make sure they don't fly out screaming. The five of them float toward the door, while I make sure to tiptoe. I slowly close the door behind me, unwrap the granola bar, and breathe a sigh of relief. "What's up, guys?" I crunch into the oat-and-honey bar.

"It's Griff. He's acting really weird here. Like he knows something we don't?" the Power Prophecy says without hesitation.

"Well, remember that Griff has that strange power that allows him to sense the essence of living beings rather well. Vizor has it too, but he hasn't been bothered by anything, it seems."

"What do you make of it, V?" Wisdom asks. "I'd like to trade notes with you, since I have powers akin to Griff and Vizor."

"Well, Griff told me that he feels nothing coming from Neona or Veniss. He described it as if they have no soul, or something to that effect."

"That's what I'm picking up too."

"What Griff can't figure out is how something like that can happen. Do any of you know?"

"Typically, when we've seen a soul being taken away from its host body," Solar starts, "the body dies off, but the soul lives on. In this case, the opposite seems to have occurred. The body lived on, but the soul died off."

"Basically, we have no idea how it's happening," Speed simplifies.

"Got it."

"Thanks for giving me Griff's notes, V," Wisdom says. "But what do you yourself think of this predicament?"

"My sensing powers are pretty average, so they're not as strong as yours or Vizor's, and especially not Griff's, but I don't think a whole lot of it. I think there's a very simple explanation here."

"Do tell."

"These people are probably traumatized to the point of numbness. They don't want to feel anything inside because doing so would cause them pain. It's a defense mechanism that I used a long time ago, back when the Unbound Evil still held Griff's family and mine hostage."

"Aha. I see. So you think this 'defense mechanism' is being used by Neona and Veniss?"

"Exactly."

"Hey, you!" A mysterious sound draws near. I look around, but can't see where it's coming from.

"Solar Prophecies! Back inside, now!"

"Yes, chosen one!" Forming a straight line, they oscillate back inside the house.

"You're mine now!"

I burst into my extreme form. "Show yourself, whoever you are!"

"I'm right in front of you. Can't you see?" the mysterious voice says.

– Dark Spirit, initiate Pure Extreme V!

– Oh, how I've missed this!

The Dark Spirit fuses with my extreme form, and my hair becomes bright crimson. My left eye changes to a deep purple. Heat, light, and dark energy emanate from my body. Pure Extreme V is back! Now, with the Dark Spirit's power, I should be able to see things I normally wouldn't be able to... Bingo! I see a ghost. It looks like the one from Commander Rod's picture.

I dash behind it and give it a nice, full-body axe kick to the head. KAPOW! It bounces off the rocky surface of the asteroid and skyrockets into the air. I jump up as it falls down and give it one nice aerial back kick to send it to the black hole.

"Good job, Dark Spirit." We revert back to normal.

"Likewise, V."

"And guess what! The granola bar is still here." I take the half-eaten bar out of my pocket and finish it while sitting on the asteroid.

I walk back inside. Everyone has finally woken up.

"Morning, everyone. You guys ready to go back to the castle?"

"Yup." Griff crosses his arms and smiles. "This time, Azilez actually did her hair in advance."

"HEY! I just started off using my paintbrush this time. It's SO much easier."

"Z? D? What did Neona say about the trees?" Vizor asks.

"Well, she said I could try, but they'd just become Ophoozi flowers. She said something about the asteroid rock combined with the black hole would transform any Earth seed into an Ophoozi flower." D flips his pickaxe around.

We meet Veniss in front of the castle gates. He seems to be as laid back as ever.

"Yo, friends. What brings you all back?"

"We came here to see if you know anything about Project Mutant. Does that name ring a bell?"

"Hmm… no, not really."

Wait, what? I thought he'd say yes for sure. Well, uh… this is awkward. What do I say now?

BLARE! BLARE! BLARE!

An alarm blasts off from inside the castle. All of us brace ourselves, except for Veniss, who's acting like he can't hear the alarm, as he still has his hands behind his head.

"What's that alarm for?" Griff asks.

"I don't know. Probably nothing too important." Veniss laughs stupidly. I'm legitimately concerned about his inability to discern an alarmed mood, given his constant happiness.

Regardless, we all rush inside the castle to see what's happening. The mutants in the foyer are panicking, dropping their wine glasses, spilling their Syrusima, and dropping their important papers onto the ground.

"Let's find Neona! She probably has a better grasp on events than Veniss does." Griff taps my shoulder. I nod and we head off for the military, as I imagine that is where the queen is when a castle-sized alarm blares.

Inside the military room, the computers that the troops were working on yesterday seem to be reforming themselves into pods. One by one, soldiers enter their designated pods as Commander Rod rushes to make sure everyone is secured. On the giant central-computer screen, a digital representation of the black hole is shown with a red dot in the center.

On the high rails in front of us, we spot Neona.

"What's going on?" I ask.

"The Phantom Pipeline has been found." She looks at me but doesn't turn her head. She jumps from the rails down to the commander.

"Men! Our enemy has finally shown their hideout's location. We shall charge forth and shut them down! Is that clear?"

"Yes, Your Majesty!" The troops salute her from inside their pods.

"Excellent. Move out!" She pounds her staff on the floor, and everyone in the room is teleported out in a flash of light. The alarm stops, and the troops, commander, and queen are flushed into the black hole.

Chapter 10
Let's Try that Again

Well, I guess that my concern for the black hole earlier was entirely moot. Turns out, it not only powers this entire place, but it's a portal to another world?

"Hmm… I'm gonna ask Veniss about this."

"Whaddup, li'l dude?" I hear Veniss's voice on a nearby asteroid. He appears to be talking to a flower.

"On second thought, maybe I'll just go inside the castle and ask one of the scientists." All of us stroll inside and walk up the stairs in the foyer to Star Security's headquarters. Below us, a few scientists are clicking away on the keyboards of the main computer. "Excuse us! Do you have a minute?"

"Ugh… Eyrl!" One of the scientists calls. "We have some inquiring minds for you." A tall, yellow, and noseless figure in a green lab coat walks out from behind the giant computer. Her arms are behind her back, but she has a gentle smile on her face.

"Ah, the guests that the queen told me about. What do you seek?" She puts her hands out, face-up.

"We were wondering how Star Security and the queen just jumped through the black hole. Is it really a black hole? Last I checked, the only things in the universe that could be transporters to other parts of space are wormholes." I put my hands against my lips to make sure she can hear me.

"Well, have humans on Earth discovered what is on the other side of a black hole?" She raises an eyebrow.

"Umm… no." We haven't even tried it.

"Well, it turns out the effects are different, based on what the hole absorbs. Initially, there is nothing inside. Then, as the hole sucks up energy, the space on the other side transforms into a new world, based on those energies." The mutants here seem incomparably more capable than people do back on Earth. I mean, first using a black hole as an energy source, but then figuring out what's on the other side of them?

"How'd you figure that out?" I ask.

"Well, something from the Space Garden was knocked into the black hole very recently, and we were able to follow its presence on the other side using this computer. We then detected many other life forms just like it. So, we concluded that it must be the Phantom Pipeline."

Oh, that must've been me knocking that ghost into next week.

"Thanks, that clears up all of my questions."

"You're welcome. Please come find me if you have any more."

"Will do."

It's been about a day since Star Security and Neona jumped into the hole, and no one has come back yet. I'm starting to worry a little. Maybe we should go in after them to make sure they're okay?

– *What do you think, Dark Spirit?*

– *I don't think it's necessary.*

– *Why's that?*

– *I'm currently detecting a swarm of life forms coming up the black* hole.

I run outside our house and see all of Star Security erupt out of the black hole like a geyser. The jumpsuited mutants begin aimlessly floating around the Space Garden, completely out of order. In the clutter, Commander Rod spots me and flies down using powers that seem to be akin to mine.

"T-there you are!" He grabs my shoulders. The dark-green military jacket he always wears is tattered to the point where you could barely tell he's a commander anymore.

"What happened in the Phantom Pipeline?" I gently put his

hands to his side.

"It was nuts… The world is shaped like a tube! And the gravity threw off all of my soldiers. And the queen is still there! And…"

"Whoa, whoa, whoa! Easy, commander, easy." I pat him on the back. "It seems like there was a lot to take in all at once."

"Oh, absolutely! And there was actually a reason that I sought you out."

"What's that?"

"Well, I saw how handily you fought that ghost out in the open the other day, and I was wondering if you would like to join Star Security for this operation."

"I don't have to wear one of those jumpsuits, do I?" I shudder.

"No."

"Oh, good. Okay, I'm in. Just let me get everyone else out too."

"Very well. Just hurry. Her Majesty's life could be in jeopardy!"

Chapter 11

The Phantom Pipeline

S PLAT! We drop like rocks, a few hundred feet from the air, onto the white mist beneath us. Commander Rod begins barking orders, and his soldiers scramble to their feet, ready for action. Z, D, Azilez, Vizor, Griff, and I transform into our chaos forms.

This entire world is cylindrical, covered with white mist, those derpy ghosts, and floating, clear bubbles. Some bubbles have lava, water, and light spiraling out of them.

"You six, without jumpsuits," one of Star Security points at us, "I shall tell you what we know about this world in the brief moments before our second operation."

"Excellent. Thank you." Vizor blinks and nods. "We're all ears."

"Okay, so this world's gravity is stronger than our own. That is because it is relative to the mist, rather than a central point. This means you'll be able to run and jump up on any part of the cylinder like it is flat ground. Also, I would stay clear from any of the bubbles. It seems that some of them are houses, but the others are, as you can see, filled with light, water, and lava. Other than that, there is not much we know."

"Knowing a little is better than knowing nothing on the battle-field." Vizor smiles.

"I suppose." The soldier relaxes. "Oh, the commander is ready. I need to get back now." He becomes uptight again and flails to his post.

"You six back there will be our lead distractions," Rod addresses my friends, brothers, and me. "Get out there and make as much noise as you can for us. At the end of this cylinder, you'll see a giant blue bubble where the queen disappeared with the leader of the Phantom Pipeline. Troops, once these six have distracted the ghosts, you will contain them. I'll fight with the distractors to ensure the queen's safe return. Understood?"

"Yes, Sir!" Everyone in the vicinity salutes the commander.

"Ready? MOVE!"

"HRRRRRAAAAA!"

The six of us split into two groups of three. On the right side of the tube are Azilez, Griff, and me, and on the left side are Vizor, D, and Z. The ghosts pile up and roll toward us like a bowling ball. Vizor takes his grappling hook out of his hair. He attaches his hair blades to each end and spins. A blue-flame tornado blows away the ghostly threats in his area. Z materializes a giant driver, jumps high, and strikes the ghosts to the bottom of the cylinder.

Star Security troops fly up to the falling ghosts, using powers similar to Veniss', and trap them inside glass bottles.

On my side, Griff's jet-engine hair flares to life, and the ghosts that are feverishly chasing us volley to some of Star Security. They promptly conceal the slightly charred ghosts.

"I'll open up a path!" Azilez flicks her golden staff into the sky. She follows it, grabs it, and slashes through the air, creating rainbow shockwaves, popping a lot of the bubbles in front of us. The ghosts are quick to dodge, though, and Azilez finds herself surrounded. Rod jumps to her aid and bear-hugs ten ghosts at once. He pile-drives them into the ground and somersaults back into the fray.

"There! I see a giant, blue portal." I point to where the white mist stops, leap, and back kick a ghost in the face.

"That's it! C'mon! We're almost there. Hrrraahhh!" Rod lets out a battle cry.

"Everything is going well over here, commander!" one of the troops calls out. "We'll settle things here."

"Excellent job!"

"Not so fast." A wall of a few hundred ghosts blocks our path. "None of you are setting one foot in this portal."

"Oh, really now?" Z raises an eyebrow. "What're you little squirts exactly doing about it? We're blowing through here like it's nothing!"

"I wouldn't get so cocky if I were you." One of the ghosts shakes its droplets. The ghosts pile up again, this time into a much bigger ball, one that covers the entire portal. "Come at us if you dare!"

As we're about to let loose, a blinding light is emitted from the portal, turning it white. Everyone in the area, including us, scatter from the sheer force.

"What just happened?" D grasps his pendulum.

The six of us, and Rod, regain our balance and fly into the portal. On the other side is a dilapidated, downward-spiraling staircase. The area seems to have the gravity of Earth. It's also made entirely of freezing metal, and it's very well-lit, despite the fact that every single light bulb is broken. We hear more commotion coming from below.

When we make it down, we find Neona and the Phantom Pipeline's leader at a standstill, both exhausted from fighting.

"Now… have you seen the true power… of the light?" Neona clutches her cramping stomach. Her visible breath vibrates.

"I… I don't think even *you* have seen it… Neona," the leader's ominous voice bellows. He has a metal body with "U.P." carved into it and an apparition's limbs. His arms are thin, but his fists are blocky. Out from the torso area, a single, swirly tail pops out, and he has two layers of double-spiked metal hair. The left side of his face is made of discharging red and blue wires, while a single black-and-red eye resides on the right.

"What a shallow thought, Unknown Phantom. Of course I have, and now it will assist me in taking your Phantom Reactor." Neona begins breathing normally.

"I will sacrifice anything for the safety of this reactor! The safety of my spirits depends on it." The Unknown Phantom pounds his fists together.

"You know your spirits have been nothing but nuisances. Either call all of them back here to this world or I take the reactor by force!" Neona pounds her staff to the ground, shattering some of the ice on the floor.

"NEVER!" The Unknown Phantom charges at the queen. D flies in and slashes at the phantom with his pendulum, sending him into the already-cracked wall.

"Hmm… this place is creepy. Let's liven it up a little." D erupts a tree from the ground under the Unknown Phantom. He skyrockets into the air and plummets back down with a glorious SLAM!

"Ngghh! Mnngh…" The Unknown Phantom passes out.

Neona strides to the reactor, disconnects the top wires, and covers it in a light that teleports it elsewhere. POOF! "Thanks for your help, D. All of Space Garden is in debt to you."

"It was my pleasure. That tree needed to be planted there!" D is focusing on the wrong thing.

"Hehe," Neona giggles. "Commander, I'd say this operation went swimmingly. Let's head back home, shall we?"

"Yes, Ma'am. Right away. Come on, everyone! One last dinner at Castle Kusondela with our guest troops, then we shall send them back to Earth."

"I'm SO down for that!" Azilez skips back up the stairs.

Chapter 12

Ghost Grudge

- GRIFF -

Mngh... I can't sleep today. Not just because my stomach is filled to the point of bursting, but also because I can't shake the feeling that my power is trying to tell me something.

I mean, sure. Neona, Veniss, and Rod are mutants, and what happened to them during Project Mutant probably traumatized them. But now I sense the Unknown Phantom, too, feels deep despair? There's something fishy going on between these two worlds, and I'm going to get to the bottom of it.

I tiptoe out of bed, grab my backpack with the Solar Prophecies inside, walk outside, and stretch my arms to get some feeling back into my body.

"Going somewhere?" AH! Oh... it's just Vizor. I thought it was one of the Phantom Pipeline's ghosts.

"What are you doing out here?"

"I could ask you the same question. I'm just thinking."

"Well, I'm going back to the Phantom Pipeline. I sense a deeper force at play here, and feel that the Unknown Phantom knows about this force. That's what I picked up when we attacked, anyway."

"Hmm. So it's not just me, then." Vizor jumps off the roof. "Good to know I haven't gone insane. And if you're going to the Phantom Pipeline to get some answers, then I'm coming with you. Wouldn't want this 'deeper force' consuming you, would we?"

"Definitely not. And thanks."

We run on the road to the castle, and jump into the black hole beneath. SWIRILLILILILIL…

Vizor and I barge through the big blue portal and go down the icy stairs to the bottom, where the Unknown Phantom is talking to some of his subjects. It seems they're in a meeting. We hide beneath the stairs so they won't see us.

"What'll you do now, Sire? Without the reactor here, this world will fizzle into nothingness."

"I know, I know." The Unknown Phantom's block fingers almost cover his entire head, which is pretty impressive considering the amount of metal hair he has. "But even if the world fades, you all won't. That's the good news I wanted to tell you."

"Oh, no. Then what's the bad news?" one of the feminine spirits says.

"It's not too bad that the reactor's gone. What's really bad is that the reactor is in Neona's hands. With it, she'll be able to execute her master plan. I cannot allow that!"

"Hold it right there!" I think now is the best time to interrupt.

"HUH? How long were you two there?"

"Long enough. What's going on?" I ask.

"This doesn't concern you. Just leave and never return. I might spare your life."

"Cut the act, Unknown Phantom. Stop pretending to be someone you're not," Vizor steps in. "That voice modulator really doesn't suit you."

"How did you know about that?" The Unknown Phantom turns off the device. "Who are you?" He now sounds like a shrill old lady.

"Griff and Vizor," I answer. "Our names are Griff and Vizor. I'm a human, and Vizor is an Omoh sapien."

"Hmm… intriguing. Still won't stop me from sending you to Hell!" But we've already been there. Bah! Forget it. She means business now.

The two of us attack her from both sides. Her ghosts try tackling us, but Vizor and I burst back into our chaos forms and shed them off like a snake's skin. Vizor takes out his grappling hook and throws one end at the Unknown Phantom. She dodges and parries my hammer fists.

"I'll admit, you two have some very familiar powers. Doesn't mean I trust you!" She pounds her fist to the ground and cracks some ice into the air. Her ghostly tail flings the shards at us. I magnify my jet-engine hair and melt all of it.

Her eye grows brighter. A dark mist fills the air. Suddenly, we can't see!

"Boo!" I get tail-swiped across my face and fly onto the icy ground. My backpack falls off. "What do we have here?" The Unknown Phantom breathes in all of the black mist, making my backpack visible.

Vizor comes in from behind and cross-slashes the phantom's back, forming an X-shaped carve. The phantom bounces back and tackles Vizor. She punches him in the face repeatedly, knocking his hair blades out of his hands.

This is my chance! I charge my right index finger with my strong sensing ability. It glows orange like a candle. I jump behind the phantom's head and touch it. It powers down.

"Whew. That was close. You okay, Vizor?" I put my hand out.

"GRRRAAAHHH!" Out of nowhere, I find huge black fists in my face. "I. WILL NOT. BE BEATEN. BY SUCH. A LAME. TRICK!"

"Oof! Eee! Ahh! Gah!"

Vizor slices at her with his blades. She careens into the wall. Vizor immediately grapples her and shoulder-tackles. When she gets sent into the air, Vizor follows above her, summons a blue tornado with his spinning hair blades, and sends her into the ground so hard that all of the surrounding ice cracks.

"Ugh…"

"Game over, Unknown Phantom." Vizor lands.

"Very well. Finish me, if you will." The wires in her body discharge more than normal.

"No," I respond.

"Huh? Why not? Isn't that why you came here? To defeat me?"

"Not at all. We wanted answers."

"For what?"

"Your despair."

"What despair? I don't know what you're talking about."

"Are you sure? I think I struck a nerve." I cross my arms.

The Unknown Phantom crawls out of the ice hole that Vizor put her in. "Fine. I guess I have no choice in the matter. I don't know how you two know of my despair, but it probably has something to do with that power of yours that I've felt before."

"You mean these?" I unzip my backpack, and the five Solar Prophecies come flying out.

"Oh, yay! AIR!" The Speed Prophecy rejoices.

"Oh, jeez. Speedy's going at it again." The Power Prophecy spins once.

"I'd let it go. Speedy will tire out like a child who's had too much sugar," Wisdom says.

Vizor summons the Shadow Prophecies from his hair blades as well.

"Where did you find these?" The Unknown Phantom lowers her eyebrows.

"That's not the hot issue right now," I fire back. "Have you seen tablets like these before?"

"Well, not any of those. The ones I saw were yellow."

"Who had them?"

"It was–"

In a flash, a beam of light surrounds us, and I'm forced to close my eyes so I don't go blind.

Chapter 13

Oops, Wrong Room

- GRIFF -

I don't really want to open my eyes. I can still see remnants of that huge flash. It's so bright on the inside of my eyelids that I can't even tell if that flash is around us or not, but a tiny peek shouldn't hurt, right?

"Huh? We're back at the castle. Vizor, open your eyes." Wait a second. Is my backpack–? Okay, it's there. Phew!

"Are you sure that's not just your eyes playing tricks on you?" Vizor keeps his palms square over his eyelids.

"Positive."

Vizor lifts his right hand and lets out a sigh of relief. "So that beam of light teleported us here? Why? And, more importantly, how?"

We're in the corridors of the upper floors, and there are doors and hallways everywhere we look. I don't remember the castle being THIS expansive. In addition, there is no sign of life anywhere. I don't like this… It's unsettling having all of this ornate carpeting. "I think it's high time we visit the queen. We need to ask her about Project Mutant before anything like this happens again."

"Sure, but where is she? These doors could lead to anything, even that odd blue room that the queen told us to stay out of."

That's right. I'd forgotten. Without the queen's power, we can't sense any decoy doors. "Let's just stay in the hallways, then. She's bound to come out of one of these doors eventually… Hopefully."

We bumble around for a while, making sure to stick together.

We press our heads against some of the doors to try and see what might be inside, but that doesn't really work because Vizor's hair blades get in the way. Doesn't he realize he can just take them off? I know I'd love to have a weapon in my hand right now. The more we venture through this lifeless castle, the more this unease inside me grows.

I sit down, bored from turning corners every five seconds.

"Griff! Isn't that her over there?" Vizor grabs my shoulder and points to the end of the current hallway. I briefly see a blue dress disappear into the next hallway. It's hard to sense her because she has no soul, but I manage to find a trace of her "presence".

"Yeah, it is! Neona, wait a second! We need to ask you about something." I push myself off the ground and dash to the next corner, and see one of the far-left doors close. "She must've gone in there." Presuming that the queen wouldn't willingly go inside one of those traps, I open the door, let Vizor inside, and slam it shut. "Neona, tell us about Project Mutant, please. Were you on that mission–"

"GRIFF, RUN! IT'S THE TRAP ROOM!" A violent wind crashes from a podium, spiraling all of the furniture in the room.

"Wait! That means the queen's in here too! We can't just leave her!"

"Is that a joke? We'll die if we stay here!"

"So will she!"

"UGH!" Vizor yanks my hand, bursts into his chaos form, and darts to the door. As we get closer, it seems to be running away from us like in a child's nightmare. Vizor speeds it up. "ALMOST… THERE!"

Poof.

Chapter 14

Phantasm Cataclysm

"V, GET UP! Vizor and Griff are gone! I can't find them any-where." Azilez yanks my shirt and shakes me. So much for a peaceful morning.

"Whoa, whoa. Calm down, girl. They probably just went to the castle early. Griff's been really itchy lately. It wouldn't surprise me."

"I checked there. Veniss says he hasn't seen them anywhere." Azilez looks like she's about to burst into tears.

"You do know Veniss tried talking to a flower, right? He probably just missed them."

"I thought that too, so I checked with the commander, and he said he hasn't seen them either. And he's got surveillance over the whole castle and its surrounding area."

Oh. Maybe something did happen, then. "Z, D. Let's–"

"Waaaaaay ahead of you, V. We helped Azilez look for 'em." Z's carrying a driver.

"COME ON! They could be in trouble. STEP ON IT!" Azilez yanks me out of bed.

"Okay, okay. I'm up." There's no stopping Azilez once her mind's set.

We step outside and see that nothing much has changed from yesterday. The yellow roads are still yellow, the castle is still standing, the black hole is still teeming with energy, and the mutants are bustling.

Until the Unknown Phantom and its ghosts come out of the hole. Uninvited, I'm assuming, because they immediately attack the castle.

"They're attacking the queen's chambers!" one of the citizens cries out. "Quick. We must protect her!" Everyone in the vicinity storms the castle. Azilez, Z, D, and I burst into our chaos forms and fly directly to the top. Our powers surge through the ghostly subjects.

"Neona, need some help?" I clench my fists.

"What are you all doing here? You need to get out of here. The phantom will destroy you!" She points her staff at us and we are teleported elsewhere.

Chapter 15

Planet Arsm

This is the queen's idea of "safe?" Well, it was all in the heat of the moment. I guess I should be thanking her, but she shouldn't try to fight all of those battles by herself. It's a lot to bear, and asking for help once in a while isn't shameful.

That aside, I don't think I've ever seen a planet with *this* hostile of an environment. The clouds in the air are as thick as tar, making it difficult to breathe. The ground is made of a dry, powdery substance that I think is dirt, but I am not touching it to find out. It's also blisteringly hot here. It's hotter than Mercury, I'd wager.

"Everyone okay?" I turn around to make sure Azilez, D, and Z are there.

"… Ooohh. I think my head hit this metal thingy here." Azilez rubs her hair. "But yeah, just dandy."

"Well, uh… what now?" I ask.

"Yeah, what now, o great chosen one?" Z crosses his arms.

"Shush, you. No, but seriously. Where are we?"

"Grrrggghhh…"

"Azilez, I know you're hungry, but please control yourself."

"That wasn't me!" Azilez pounds her staff against her chest.

"Grghlghl!" I look at the metal-scrap hill in front of me, and see a patched-up, oxidized pile of titanium trudging toward us.

As I prepare to blast it into the hill, someone jumps out from behind the metal monstrosity and slices it in half with her flowing, blond hair.

"Whew... more of these things have been popping up every-where. You guys okay?" She appears to be a human. That's good. It must mean we're somewhere on Earth! But what place on Earth looks like construction-zone hell?

"Yes! Thanks, lady!" D runs up to give her a hug.

"Oh, no no no no, stay back." The girl puts her left palm out. D comes to a halt. "I'm not normal. You could end up like me if you touch me."

"But your hair just now was awesome!" Azilez compliments. "Love the outfit too! It screams 'APOCALYPSE.'" Not sure if that was a compliment, but, yeah, her clothes are definitely worn. Her tank top is shaved off at the bottom, and the left shoulder band is gone. One side of her jeans is intact, while the other has almost completely torn off. She's barefoot, which is impressive, considering she's standing on scrap metal and has deep scars scattered throughout the upper half of her body.

"Thanks?" She raises an eyebrow. "Anyway, I'm Aria, and I've completely lost hope."

"That's pretty melodramatic. You sure you want that on your business card?" Z asks.

"Trust me when I say it's my only viable option." Aria looks di-rectly at Z. "I didn't want to live on this forsaken planet, but now I'm here. There's nothing for me to do but explore ruins and fight the enemy I can never find."

"Fight the enemy? You mean those metal creeps?" Azilez asks.

"No. It's over there." She turns around and points, revealing a tall mountain. "A beast lives there on Mount Marsmite. I'm trying to find and kill it, but I can't even find it. Do you guys mind helping me?"

"A beast? Sure. But, question."

"What?"

"Where are we?" I ask.

"Arsm. You are on Arsm."

"What galaxy are we in?" I keep asking.

"I have no idea." Aria rolls her eyes.

I stop asking questions, mainly because I can't stand to hear her whining. It's constant, and she sounds bored all the time. She's right. I don't want to be like her. But... if she knows her attitude sucks, why not change it?

We arrive at the base of the mountain. "Okay, so where do you generally look to find this beast?" No answer. "Aria?" Still no answer. I look back. "Where'd she go? Azilez, did you see her wander off?"

"Nope."

"D?"

"No."

"Okay, then."

As I'm about to start ascending the mountain, Z interrupts: "Hey, why didn't you ask me?"

"Because I already know your answer."

"Why's that?"

"You were spending the whole time looking for a place that would make a good golf course."

"Quite observant of you."

"Is it observing when you fly circles around me, in an attempt to get a better view? Never mind. Let's just go."

The base of the mountain is steep, but it's nothing we can't fly over. Once the incline starts easing off, I sense ten powerful, familiar presences nearby. The prophecies! Then that must mean...

"Griff and Vizor are nearby. I can feel it."

"Oh, good. Now I can slap them both for making me worry so much!" At least Azilez has her priorities straight.

"Beast first. Slapping later," Z says.

"Fine."

We spot a mine cart that leads into a tunnel, and hop in. The track drops down like a roller coaster and flies off the track for a little, only to land on another track that curves around and immediately stops in front of a spring. After jumping in, I sense the prophecies are farther down the mountain. The four of us swim down, careful not to touch the metal lining of the pool. Once we hit the bottom, we see that the spring branches off into a tunnel.

The tunnel starts off with water inside, but then goes a little north again, leading us to dry land. We follow a path spiraling into a hot chamber. Steam rises and erupts, forcing us upward. We now find ourselves at the peak of the mountain.

At the very tip of the mountain, there is a giant hole. In it, I sense the prophecies, Griff, and Vizor. We jump down.

Quaking the ground, we land in a pitch-dark place, lit only by the energy of our chaos forms.

"Oh, guys! Good thing you're all here," Griff says. "We need to fight off the beast."

"Wait, how'd you guys get here?" D asks. "Where is the beast?"

"KEKEKEKE… RIGHT HERE." A dead, robotic sound bellows. We hear a metal-on-metal screeching sound from every corner of the pit we're in.

"She's coming back!" Vizor takes out his hair blades.

"She?" I ask. "You know who the beast is?"

"Of course! It's Aria."

Chapter 16

The Vanity Prophecies

How can Aria be the beast if that's what she's chasing?

"KEKEKE... MORE SOULS TO FEAST ON!" Aria bursts out from beneath the surface, her hair swirling as fast as a hurricane. Her smile is abnormally big and is constantly shaking. The scars on her upper body glow with some sort of yellow energy. Her once-empty irises are now layered with several black rings.

And just like with Neona and Veniss, even with this piercing presence, I can't sense her soul anywhere.

"What happened to you? You were so collected a few minutes ago! A bit bratty, but nothing compared to THIS." I throw my hands out, unable to describe what's in front of me.

"FOOLS! I'VE BEEN ENLIGHTENED BY THE LIGHT. NOW, I WILL CONSUME EVERY LAST ONE OF YOU!" I think her definition of "enlightened" is a bit skewed. Just a bit. She spins her head around, causing some of the metal pit to break off. While the debris is in the air, she slices through it with her hair, like a piece of paper going through a shredder.

SCCCRREEEEEEEEEEEECCHHH!

"OW! My ears!" Azilez kneels down and claps her hands onto the sides of her head to keep out the infernal noise. "How did she do that? That piece was solid metal!" The winds from Aria's hair grow stronger.

"Her hair must be made of metal also." Vizor deducts. "Or something even sharper. Stay away from it, at all costs!"

"KEKEKEKE... LET'S HAVE A FUN TIME! IT'LL BE YOUR LAST!"

Aria flies into the mountain at supersonic speeds, using her hair as a makeshift propeller. For a moment, it grows quiet. Then we hear the faint sounds of an avalanche.

Griff places his index finger on his forehead to try and sense where she is. "Aria's on the side of the mountain."

"Then we're going up." Z flies out of the pit, to the top of the mountain, to get a better view. We follow. "All right, ya psycho. Try outrunning my driver. FORE!" Z snaps and a giant golf ball drops in front of him. Before it even makes contact with the ground, Z smacks it into the horizon. "Everyone, go as high as you can. You wouldn't want to get caught in this." I think I see what he's trying to do. All of us rise to the thick clouds.

I look in the opposite direction of where he hit the ball. It loops around the entire planet and comes back on fire, getting faster and faster. The ball is moving around the planet so fast that not only is it on fire, but it's spewing out flames everywhere.

Aria looks up, completely unaware of the ball in the sky, until an ember drops on her already-distorted skin. She stops her little scheme and propels her hair at the embers. I can't imagine why she'd do that. I mean, she's trying to use metal to shield herself from a fireball? That's about as fail-safe as using a twig to block a gunshot.

Wait, hold on. She's not burning? Oh. Ohhhh. That's not good. The flames infuse with her hair, and now she can shoot fire from her metal hair. Irony. It finds a way.

Noticing this, Z strikes the comet ball out of the sky and at Aria. Her hair completely destroys it.

"I LOVE TO TOY WITH MY FOOD BEFORE I EAT IT… MAKES CATCHING IT EVEN MORE SATISFYING!" She charges at all of us. We disperse in different directions. D summons a tree from the sky to fall on her. Aria shreds it. She tries to catch him, but D blows her away in a vortex of green razor petals.

Vizor squeezes himself and melts into a puddle – a classic Omoh sapien ability. He waits for Aria to fly over him, rematerializes, grabs her ankle, and flings her into a nearby scrap-metal hill. Aria breaks free, scattering the debris she created with her hair. Vizor melts it all with the black flames on his blades.

Aria confronts Azilez, who is still struggling to hear anything from the screech earlier. Azilez points her scepter at Aria and fires a gargantuan scoop of rich, thick vanilla ice cream at her. She tries to fend it off with her hair but can't this time. The ice cream dowses the flames on her hair, and it stops spinning.

"Let me give you a crash course in food, Aria." Azilez launches a massive plastic cup to trap the ice cream inside. "All right. Here's how you make an ice cream sundae. Step one's done. Step two, hot fudge." Azilez treats her scepter like a bottle and pours ooey-gooey chocolate fudge on top of the single scoop. "Step three, sprinkles and chopped almonds." She goes on top of the sundae and adds those manually. "And, finally, the cherry on top!" She waves her scepter in the air, and a super-sized cherry falls into her left hand. Using all the energy she can muster, Azilez leans back, winds up, and SPLAT! The sundae explodes and Aria tumbles back.

Though, that does not stop her. If anything, she's just even angrier now. Her iris' black circles turn red, and her hair starts spinning again. "ENOUGH TOYING… MY HUNGER GROWS!"

After taking a bite of Azilez's sundae, I find Aria zooming around the metal hills, chewing and spitting out bit-sized debris faster than a machine gun. Using the Dark Spirit's power, I change from my chaos form to my dark form.

"If she's obsessed with the light so much, then she'll be disappointed to find out that not everything revolves around the light."

I sneak underground, trying to find an opening. Her feet seem to be the best approach. Her spinning hair makes anything from behind impossible, while that machine-gun mouth makes anything from high up dangerous too.

"Whoa!" She swipes at me in the ground and I fly out just in time to avoid a major flesh wound.

"DON'T YOU KNOW, V? THE LIGHT ALWAYS CASTS A SHADOW. IT SEES EVERYTHING."

– We were invisible! How did she see us?

– I don't know. It seems highly improbable that someone without a soul would be able to sense others with one! She must have some sort of power source.

"KRRRAAHH!" She rushes me down, trying to cut me with her hair as much as possible. I disappear into the planet, but she follows. Eventually, I reach its core, where there's an open, blazing area and a dense metal sphere in the center. "UGH..." Aria holds her forehead.

– Dark Spirit, I think the intense magnetic field is messing with her.

– Get her closer to the core. Her hair will stick onto it.

As I fly, I lay out dark spheres for her to dodge, encouraging her to catch me. Ever so slightly, every time I go around the core, I edge closer to it. Within minutes, Aria can't handle the magnetic field anymore, and her hair causes her head to crash into the core. If that didn't faze her, then this will!

Now that I know she can't whirl her hair, I wind up an axe-kick, and, BAM! Aria comets through the whole interior of the planet and back to the surface, unconscious.

"V!" Griff finds me after I resurface.

"Hey, buddy. Where've you been?"

"We're in trouble."

"Why?"

"I sensed five incredibly powerful presences underneath the pit we were in on Mount Marsmite. I went to check what they were, but before I could open the chamber door, five dark-yellow tablets flew out of the room! Aria has her own set of prophecies, and I think they just sensed that she's in pain."

"How can someone as twisted as her have a set of prophecies dedicated to her?" I wonder.

"I think there are too many things we don't know here. And I feel like Aria is the key to figuring it all out."

"How are you so sure about this?"

"I sense something locked away inside Aria. Her soul is there, but it's very faint. I'd even say almost gone, but if we can snap her out of this psycho state somehow, she'll have a chance to get her soul back."

"Sounds good to me."

"KEKEKEKEKE... YOU THINK I'M DONE WITH YOU?" A voice echoes from behind Mount Marsmite. Aria jumps out and impacts the ground so profoundly that she shatters it. It's nothing Griff and I haven't seen, though. We're unaffected by it. I transform back into my chaos form. "NOW YOU'LL SEE THE TRUE POWER OF THE VANITY PROPH-ECIES!" The five prophecies Griff was talking about appear from behind Aria. They don't seem to be able to talk like Vizor's Shadow Prophe-cies. Griff was right. The force coming from them is overwhelming. It's even greater than the pressure I felt in the planet's core. Mount Marsmite erupts light. It falls around us, creating a barrier. "NOW THERE'S NO RUNNING FOR YOU. NO ICE CREAM, NOTHING! NOTHING WILL STOP MY TITANIUM HAIR FROM DESTROYING YOU BOTH!"

"Do your worst!" Griff clenches his fists.

"Get that girl, Griff! V!" The Speed Prophecy hugs the outside of the barrier like it's a boxing cage. The other four Solar Prophecies are behind it.

Aria rushes at us immediately. Griff hammers into the ground. I follow him. We see if there is a way to go under the barrier, but it's no good. The barrier runs deep in the planet. I shoot white fireballs from my palms at Aria. Since her hair is propelling her forward, she can't use them to absorb the fireballs, and they hit her, square in the arms.

"AAAAAAAAAHHHHHHHH!" Her demonic scream rings through-out the planet's interior. The resulting tremor causes such a disturbance that magma seeps to the surface and begins devouring all of the metal on the planet. Pretty soon, the entire planet will be flooded in lava. We rise to the surface, where the barrier remains standing. "YOU WILL SUFFER! THE DARKNESS WILL NOT LET YOU HIDE ANYWHERE! THE LIGHT WILL SNIFF YOU OUT AND CONSUME YOU!"

"Why are you so insistent that the light alone will show you the way?" I ask.

"IT CAN SEE ALL. THEREFORE IT KNOWS ALL."

"Then how will the light explain this?" *Dark Spirit, be ready to recharge me. This is going to use all of my energy.*

– Ready, V!

I fuse the Dark Spirit's energy with my evil form's energy to create Void V.

"PLEASE! THIS IS NOTHING MY HAIR CAN'T TEAR THROUGH!"

I show her my palm. "Black-hole bomb!" Griff closes his ears. A huge black sphere engulfs Aria and dissolves the barrier of light. In a glorious supernova, the bomb explodes, taking the planet, Aria, and the Vanity Prophecies with it. I fly around the Solar Prophecies, making sure they do not veer off into unknown territory. Azilez, Vizor, D, and Z spot Griff and me. I revert to my normal self. But I barely have enough energy to stand.

"One second… There you go, V. Your body should be recharged now."

"Whew. Thanks!"

"Now for the moment of truth." Griff flies up to the unconscious, floating Aria, who somehow has survived the blast. "Everyone, put your hands on her forehead. Her memories should be surging in any second now."

Chapter 17

Second-grade Issues
TEN YEARS AGO – ARIA

"So as you can see, kids, two times three is six." A clear example is written on the chalkboard.

"Ugh! This is the same lesson as yesterday. Why are we learning it again?" I pull my soft, brown hair.

"Aria, is there a problem?"

"No, Ms. Cassidy. Sorry…" I slam my head against my wooden desk.

Recess comes around, and I look for Neon and Vanessa. Those two always seem to get in trouble, even though it's normally not their fault. Every school they transfer to, their classmates just think they're too… how do I put this nicely… eccentric.

"Check it out, Neon! I found a big one this time. And it's green."

"Oh! Oh! Lemme see."

There they are. I was starting to worry. Seems no one is bothering them. That's good.

Vanessa and Neon are siblings, and you could tell by their vast similarities. Both love bug hunting, have freckles and white hair, and they even skip around the field almost identically. If Vanessa were not wearing pigtails, you could not even tell the two apart. You would think they are twins, but trust me when I say they are not.

I would know. Vanessa has been my best friend since birth. We love doing everything together – eating, walking, playing, doing home-work, you name it.

"See? It's disgusting, right?" Vanessa holds up a beetle like it's a gold trophy.

"Eww! Yeah, it's awesome! Probably the biggest one we've ever found." Neon reaches for it, but Vanessa goes on her tiptoes to stop him.

"Nyeh-ni-nyeh-ni-nyeh-nyeh! You can't get it. I'm too tall."

"Right, like that'll help you." Neon tickles her underarms.

"Ahahaha! No! No! I'm gonna drop it." Vanessa throws the bee-tle away from the tickle fest to prevent it from getting hurt. As Neon continues tickling, they move closer to the beetle, and Vanessa crushes it under her muddy shoes. "Doh! Now look what you've done, Neon."

"What *I've* done? You crushed it!"

"You started tickling me!"

"Maybe you should stop being so ticklish!"

"Maybe you should stop tickling!"

"Hey, hey. There's no need to fight here, guys." It was only a matter of time before trouble would show up. This happens every day. I watch from my hiding spot behind the jungle gym.

"What do YOU want?" Vanessa scrunches her nose and points at the three oversized kids.

"To play with the bugs and you guys," one of them replies, crack-ing his knuckles.

"Really?" Vanessa actually believes them.

"Yeah, here. I'll help you get a better look at them." A boy pushes her into the mud, face first. Another approaches Neon. Paralyzed with fear, he just sits there closing his eyes and pushing his hands out, knees shaking.

"Hey! You three. Scram." I stand from my kneeling position.

"It's Aria! RUN!"

"Just wait, you two. One day, your little friend won't be there to protect you." They buzz off.

I rush to Vanessa. "Are you okay?"

"*Pffft*... I think so."

"Come on. Let's get you cleaned up." I have been taking karate ever since I learned to walk. I can protect Neon and Vanessa – which is why they rarely ever get hurt – but that does not stop their classmates from teasing them.

I escort Vanessa and Neon to the bathroom. Neon goes into the boys', while I help Vanessa into the girls'. I dispense some paper towels and get them damp. As I wash Vanessa's skin, she starts bawling… again.

"What is wrong, Vanessa?" As if I don't know.

"*Sniffle*… Why do people keep being mean to me?"

I grab her now-spotless shoulders. "Because they're jealous. Jealous that they're not as cool and awesome as you."

"You're just saying that! Everywhere I go, bullies go too." She has a point. We've transferred schools three times now, and Neon and her keep getting picked on. Hmm…

"And who else follows you around everywhere you go?" I raise an eyebrow.

"Who?" She looks up, her green eyes magnified by her tears.

"Neon and me, silly." I shake her hair, which I know she loves.

"Teehehee!" She wipes her eyes with her muddy hands. I immediately clean both. Her smile reveals her two lost front teeth.

We continue to our next class with Neon and finish the day. Pretty average for us, if I do say so myself – lessons I cannot stand, bullies trying to pick on Vanessa and Neon, and me warding them off.

That is, until Vanessa suggests something crazy.

Chapter 18

Desperate Times, Desperate Measures
TEN YEARS AGO – ARIA

"I'm sorry, say that again, Vanessa?" I raise my head from the velvet-cushioned chair.

"We should live in space! There are no bullies there." She pulls out a half-torn poster from her backpack. It says that the US government is looking for 5,000 volunteers to go to the first Mars mission, to see if life can be sustained there. It also says that each volunteer would be paid 20,000 dollars.

"Vanessa, if it'll make you happy, then it'll make us happy too." Vanessa's mom walks into the dining room.

"Go for it, sweetheart. I don't see why not." Vanessa's dad follows. This is the one thing that bothers me about Vanessa: her parents. They let her do anything she wants. It is not like I can tell her parents that they are stupid. But going to Mars is a pretty big change. I should probably speak up.

"Um… not to sound pessimistic, but is not going to space a bit too much?"

"W-what do you mean?" Vanessa freezes.

"Well, we could just transfer schools again, right? Or how about moving to a different state? It will be much simpler than launching ourselves into space. Or why don't you take karate classes with me?"

"No! I want to go to space now!" Vanessa stomps her foot on the ground. Her parents throw her a piece of Laffy Taffy to calm her down.

"Of course, dear. We won't have anyone tell you no. Security!" Vanessa's mom calls out.

"Wait. What?" Two enormous men grab each of my arms, walk out the silver front door, and throw me over the iron fence.

"Well, that wasn't good. My best friend's going to space, and I'm getting left behind. Unless... I go too! My parents will say yes, right?"

"Absolutely not, Aria." My dad crosses his arms.

"Oh, come on! Why?"

"Listen to yourself. 'I want to go to Mars and live with my best friend.' I get she means a lot to you, but you'll just have to deal with it." I can always count on my dad to smack some reality into me. It does sound insane, now that I think about it. But still... does Vanessa not realize that others, too, will be on that ship? Her situation will not change just because of a change in scenery.

"Okay, then. Can we at least go the day of the launch so I can say bye to Vanessa?"

"Fine."

Chapter 19

Launch Base

TEN YEARS AGO – ARIA

I think this is the most people I've ever seen in any one area.

I would say it is overkill, but then I realize this is the first human mission to Mars. The more I think about it, the more this crowd actually benefits me because I can squirm my way to the rocket.

Oh, I do not plan on boarding the rocket. I just want to speak with Vanessa. She needs to know that her life here is not as bad as she thinks. Sure, school is terrible, but there is much more to a kid's life than school. I have to beg. It is my only chance to get her to stay.

All right. My parents get bumped over by the rushing crowd. Go time!

"And we're standing outside what might just be the greatest moment in history," a reporter speaks into a microphone. "Live from the Kennedy Space Center in Florida, it's the first-ever US mission to Mars!" I try my best to avoid the reporter at all costs, but the flow of the crowd pushes me toward him. "Excuse me, little girl. What do you have to say about this moment in history?"

"No time! I am in a hurry."

I shove past the reporter and fight the crowd ahead. Since I am much smaller than most of them (being in second grade and all), I mainly just have to push against their legs. Not that I am comfortable with that. There were some very hairy legs in that crowd... Yuck!

There she is! I wave to her.

"What are you doing here?" Vanessa has a spring in her step. She is practically skipping onto the rocket. Neon goes ahead of her.

"Vanessa… PLEASE DO NOT GO! I WILL BE MISERABLE WITH-OUT YOU!" I get on my knees and bow to her like she is a queen.

"Then come with me. You won't be alone then."

"What? No! You need to come back. Life here is not…"

"Hey, what are you doing there? Get back in line!" one of the scientists scolds me. She grabs me by my left arm. I resist, kick, and flail, but she throws me next to Vanessa anyway.

"MOM! DAD! HELP ME!"

It is no use. I cannot even see them in the sea of people.

Chapter 20
Project Mutant
SIX YEARS AGO - ARIA

It is about time we got to Mars. I stopped asking "Are we there yet?" years ago. That ship was slow, but at least I am here now.

Dressed in my white jumpsuit, I walk into the spacecraft's laboratory to receive the suit I will need to go to Mars. That is when I freeze, as I spot two faces I thought I would never see again.

"Nocturne? Prismo? You guys jumped on too? What are you doing here?"

"'Course we did. We knew what you were up to, little Miss sneakaway-with-my-best-friend." Prismo acts all cocky.

"It was not like that! This was an accident. Okay? An accident. It just happened to be this way, got it?"

"Yeah, Prismo, cool your jets. It's not like Aria to just abandon everything on Earth and come here."

"Thank you, Nocturne." I bow my head quickly.

"No need for the formalities. We're all familiar with each other, aren't we?"

"Not exactly. I have not seen either of you in four years."

"Well, with scientists this strict, it was possible to keep us apart, I guess," Nocturne assumes.

"Yeah! Can you believe the nerve on these guys? I couldn't even get dessert last night because I was 'too loud.'" Prismo uses his fingers as quotation marks.

"But how about you, sisty? How are you? And Vanessa?" Yup. That's Nocturne, for sure. No one else calls me that.

"I am fine, but I am not too sure about Vanessa. She seems depressed every day, and I have no idea what to do about it."

"Seems depressed? How so?"

"Well, it started when we found out we were bunking with her grandmother, Orient…"

"Hey, you three! Into the lab." We shrug and walk in, used to the scientists' stuck-up behavior.

In the lab, I don't see spacesuits anywhere. What I do see are giant glass tubes filled with a multicolored liquid and a line of people waiting to be seated in a single, intensely lit chair with straps on it.

"Uhh… where are the suits?" I ask one of the scientists. He just ignores me and walks to the front of the line.

"You first," I hear.

"No! Please! NO!" That is Vanessa! She is up front? What are they going to do to her? I would step in, but my muscles feel weak from being stuck in that spaceship for four years, and I have forgotten most of my karate training. I have not had to fight anyone in a long time.

"Now, now. Let's not get ahead of ourselves," Orient's old voice comes up. "You've waited four years for this moment. What's a little longer?" I see her give a bag of coins to each of the scientists trying to grab Vanessa. They take her to the back of the line, where we are.

"Thank goodness you are o–"

CHCHCHHCHCHCHZZZZZZZZZZZCHCHCHCHCZZZZ….

MMMMMMMMMRRRRRFFFF…!

I have no idea what those sounds are, but I look up to find out. That is probably the biggest mistake I have ever made. I see Orient strapped to the chair. Multicolored lightning bolts strike her on every part of her body. Her mouth is taped shut so we can't hear her scream.

At that moment, I realize that soon that is going to happen to us too. I grab my head, trying to comprehend what that might feel like. But my brain cannot imagine something so cruel.

CHCHCHHCHCHZZZZZZZZZZZCHCHCHCHCZZZZZ....

I am trying to picture it in my mind, but... it is going numb. I cannot feel anything. I do not *want* to feel anything. Not when all I have to feel is...

CHCHCHHCHCHZZZZZZZZZZZCHCHCHCHCZZZZZ....

Sounds... they're in my head now. Fufufufu... get out. Get out. Get out. Get out. Get out. Get out. Get out. Get out. Get out. Get out. Get out. Get out. Get out. Get out. Get out. Get out. Get out. Get out. Get out.

CHCHCHHCHCHZZZZZZZZZZZCHCHCHCHCZZZZZ....

I am getting closer to the chair. Or is it getting closer to me?

CHCHCHHCHCHZZZZZZZZZZZCHCHCHCHCZZZZZ....

I see corpses lying everywhere. They are piling up like mountains. I see corpses lying everywhere. They smell like home to me. I see the chair, right in front of me. I feel the straps on my arms. They are so warm, but is it the feeling of life? Blood? Death? Who cares? What use is life when all I can see is death?

CHCHCHHCHCHZZZZZZZZZZZCHCHCHCHCZZZZZ....

AAAAaaaaaAAAAAAAAaaaaaaaaaaaaHHHHHHHH!

UuuuuuuuuurrrrrrrGGGGGGGGGGGGGhHhHhHhllllLLLLl!

Was that me screaming? Or was that death's language? I'll never know. My mouth was taped shut. How should I know who was screaming? Was that scream even real? Or was that just the noise in my head? Getting louder. Louder. Louder. Louder. LOUDER. LOUDER. LOUDER! LOUDER!! LOUDER!!!

But then there is silence. Sweet, sweet silence. Oh, how I have longed for you. Where have you been all this time? Have you been comforting Orient? Or is her afterlife filled with noise? Wait... where are you going? What do you mean "No?" Take me there. TAKE ME, PLEASE! I WANT MY SUFFERING TO END.

CHCHCHHCHCHZZZZZZZZZZZCHCHCHCHCZZZZZ....

Brothers...? Those are not my brothers. They are just freaks with fine titanium hair like me. Why, though? Why are we the fruitless creations of human greed? Why could it not have been the noises in my head? Why? Why? Why? WHY? WHY? WHY? WHY? WHY? WHY? WHY?

WHYWHYWHYWHYWHYWHYWHYWHYWHYWHYWHYWHY?
Why. Why… Why…

CHCHCHHCHCHZZZZZZZZZZCHCHCHCHCZZZZZ….

Not Vanessa too. She is still smiling, though. That is peculiar. I wonder what she is smiling about. Maybe it is her new pale skin? Or the blond hair? Or her yellow eyes? Even with her body totally changed, she is the only thing I recognize.

CHCHCHHCHCHZZZZZZZZZZCHCHCHCHCZZZZZ….

Get out. GET OUT.

CHCHCHHCHCHZZZZZZZZZZCHCHCHCHCZZZZZ….
CHCHCHHCHCHZZZZZZZZZZCHCHCHCHCZZZZZ….
CHCHCHHCHCHZZZZZZZZZZCHCHCHCHCZZZZZ….

Hehehehehe… HEHEHEHEHEHE… HAHAHAHAHAHAHA! The sounds… the sounds are still here. Silence, take them. Take them. Release me. Embrace me. Comfort me. Comfort her. Comfort him. And him. Kill them. Kill them. Kill them. KILL THEM. KILL THEM. KILL THEM. KILL THEM. KILL THEM.

Kill me.

Chapter 21

The Only One Left
SIX YEARS AGO – ARIA

BRRRRRRIIIIIINNNGGGG!
BRRRRRRIIIIIINNNGGGG!
BRRRRRRIIIIIINNNGGGG!
BRRRRRRIIIIIINNNGGGG!

Oh, goodie. More sounds. More sounds to attract the silence!

"Do not let him get away!"

Wait. Reality? Hold on. Am I conscious? I pinch myself to make sure what I think is true, and to pull my mind together after... that episode.

Both of my brothers are next to me, still unconscious. Vanessa has gone, though. I hope she is, at least, not in the hands of any more scientists.

"He's trying to get into the escape-pod room. Close it down!" I hear another scientist's voice in the distance. I rush into the hall and almost faint at the sight of dozens of dead scientists on the cold floor. Almost. I run past them. I find the escape-pod room, along with a hefty man with flowing, silver hair. There are scientists in there with green syringes. I pretend to lie dead on the floor so none of them notice me.

With my motionless eyes open, I see this man exert beams of fierce light from his mouth and eyes. They are so powerful that I hear the sounds of bodies popping. In the aftermath, all of the scientists disappear, along with their syringes. The man looks back at me. I quickly close my eyes before he spots me. He runs past me to the spacecraft's control room, where everyone is also dead. He takes the controls and tries crash-landing into a mountain. I grab my brothers and jump off, just in time to avoid the impact. When I land, I see Vanessa and Neon, both lying unconscious on the surface of Mars.

Chapter 22

Garden of the Milky Way
SIX YEARS AGO - ARIA

"Nocturne? Prismo? Come on, please wake up." I shake their motionless bodies on the red dust, kicking some of it into my mouth.

"Ugh…" Prismo holds his head. "Aria? Is that you?"

"Yes, of course! You do not recognize me?"

"Your hair's changed." Nocturne sits up with his arm over his knee.

"What?" I grab my head and pull my hair down. It is blond now, and it feels… different. Like it is not hair anymore. It is cold. What did those scientists do to me?

Calm down, calm down. We do not want another episode like on the ship, right? Deep breaths… deep breaths. Whew. Okay.

"You are not hurt, are you?" I look at both of them.

"Don't worry 'bout it." Prismo stands. "I feel fine. A little too fine, actually."

"What does that mean?" I ask.

"Haven't you noticed we're on Mars?"

"Of course."

"How are we breathing?"

I cannot believe I am about to say this, but Prismo is right. No humans should ever be able to breathe in space, right?

"It was probably a result of the experiments. I'm just glad we all made it out of there alive."

"Did we, though? Neon and Vanessa still aren't moving."

"Oh, boy... shouldn't have said that, Nocturne."

"Neon! Vanessa!" I run at them, but something crash-lands right in front of me, sending me back to my brothers. I knock them over like bowling pins. As I rub the red, coarse dust out of my eyes, I see the man who killed those scientists in the escape-pod room!

Oh, no. Is he going to kill us too now? He is walking this way. His stomping footsteps are bringing up very familiar noises.

CH... CH... CH... Ch...

No! Stop! I am in control now. That horrible scene is behind me. There is no way anything like it could happen again.

"You three. Who are you?" Ohhh... my spine just froze. Those gold eyes stare right through me. His deep voice is commanding, and I am compelled to answer it.

"My name is Aria. And these are my brothers, Nocturne and Prismo."

"Have you been experimented on?"

"Yup. Seems our hair has changed and we can breathe in space now."

"Hmm..." He squints, as if he is looking for something specific on our faces, like a mole or something. "It seems so. You have suffered much, haven't you?"

"Umm... yes?" How else do I respond to that? It was rather forward.

"At any rate, the vessel is crushed. There is no way we will be able to set up anything here. It seems as if this 'project' was really a trap."

"We already know that, sir," a voice comes from behind. It is Neon, and Vanessa is behind him! Oh, thank goodness!

"Vanessaaaaaaa!" I jump on her and give her a hug. She does not react at all, and just keeps walking forward. I let go and stand next to my brothers again, but not before looking back at her. She barely has an expression in her now-yellow eyes, and she is frowning. Her hair has grown a lot, and it has turned yellow too. Poor Vanessa. What did those scientists do to her after they were done with me? She was the only one after me. I could not see anything they were doing. If only I had not lost my mind! I might have been able to protect her.

"But what exactly can we do about it? We have no ship, no means of transportation, and no way to call for help. We are just gonna stay here until we die."

"That would be an unfortunate fate. I will not allow it! All of you have already suffered by the hands of those humans long enough."

"Wait, what do you mean 'those humans?' You're not human?"

"Ah… er… well… no, I'm not."

"You look like one, though. What are you?" Neon asks. His mutations came with a toothbrush haircut and a change in hair color, but, other than that, he's basically the same. Odd that he and Vanessa turned out so differently.

"A… an alien! That's it. I'm just a plain ol' alien."

My mind is erratic right now, but even I can tell he is fishing for an answer.

"No specific kind of alien? You don't have a race or anything?"

"W-what? Of course not!"

He is a pretty bad liar, but why are we pressuring him when he can kill us anytime? I will just buy it.

"When you said you would not allow us to just sit here and die, did you mean you can actually do something about it?"

"Can I? Come here. Hold on to my hair, everyone."

"WHAAAA!" He flies to the nearby asteroid belt in mere minutes.

"Okay. Now go inside that cave over there. You might fly off otherwise."

"Uhh… okay." At this point, I really think he is trying to help us. I mean, he could have just tossed us out while flying here.

We huddle inside a small cave. In an instant, we are pushed back to the very end. I think the asteroid is moving. It is either that or an earthquake. I will take my chances. After all, they cannot get much lower than they already are. With my body violated like this, I would not mind dying so much…

No! There I go again. I cannot think that. I have to stay strong – if not for myself, then definitely for Vanessa. Just try to think of Vanessa.

Ahh... I remember this one winter day. There was a ton of rain outside, so she and I could not leave the house. We ran upstairs to sit on a beanbag chair and do our homework. We had hot cocoa in our hands, but Vanessa fell off the chair and it spilled all over her homework. She started crying about the destroyed homework, so I gave her mine to make her feel better. I was content. Seeing her smile was worth the zero on a ten-point assignment. It was that smile's brilliance that kept me going. I wish I could see it again someday.

The moving stops, and the mysterious man finds us. "You guys can come out now. I have a surprise for you."

A little excited and a little nervous, I step outside the dark cave. I gasp.

Even Vanessa's eyes widen. She cries a little. We seem to be in another asteroid system, but one of the asteroids is directly above a black hole and houses an enormous castle with ten spiraling bases.

"What is that?" Vanessa finally speaks.

"Your castle, Your Highness." The man kneels before Vanessa and places a sparkling crown on her head. He also hands her some sort of twisted staff made out of asteroid rock.

"R-really? It's all mine?" She finally smiles again.

"Absolutely. And this is your kingdom. Make whatever you desire of it. Everything you will need is in there."

"How did you do that, sir?" Neon asks.

"It's like I said before. I'm a plain ol' alien. I can do things that humans can't comprehend."

"But THAT quickly? There's no way you built that right when we got here."

"Ahahaha! You underestimate me, little boy."

"Wooooooow! So we can all live there?" Everyone huddles around the strange man like he's Santa Claus. I mean, he did basically just give all of us a new home.

"That was very kind of you, er… what is your name?" I ask.

He stutters again. "Uh… Rod. That's my name. Rod."

"Well, thank you, Rod. This is where we part. Come on, everyone."

"Wait!" He holds his hand out.

"Yes?" Vanessa turns her head.

"I'm actually really tired. Can I stay at the castle for one night?"

"Yeah, sure. It's the least I can do to repay you. Make yourself at home!" Vanessa pounds her new staff on the floor, and a beam of light bursts out of the staff. Rod barely ducks in time to avoid it. Actually, scratch that. It hits one of his strips of hair, and now it looks shorter than the others.

"Wha-what was that?" Vanessa's eyes become expressionless again. She shakes.

"Vanessa, do not worry. This is our home. No one, and nothing, will hurt you here." I wrap my arms around her.

It is no good! No matter what I try, it seems like she is just ignoring me now. What has gotten into her?

Chapter 23

The Starlight Prophecies
SIX YEARS AGO - ARIA

LOVE THIS CASTLE. The vastness of it makes me want to keep exploring it to see what I can find. Every time I walk into a room, I leave a sticky note on the doorstep.

I have found 15 bathrooms, 20 bedrooms, ten pantries, a full-sized golf course, 50 Olympic-sized swimming pools, 12 movie theaters, 30 concession stands loaded with snacks, 10,000 acres of farmland, and Vanessa's room, which is at the very top of the castle.

And I still have more to go! I am going to tackle the lower levels of the castle today, since I have been busy with the upper floors for the past few days.

Let me see. I think I will go through… this one! I twist the golden doorknob and I see a long, dark hallway with a light at the end. Maybe it is a storage room? I mean, there is nothing in here. There is hard tile on the floor, but that is it. I run to the light to see what could be over there. I see it is another door, but this one has a different design than all of the other ones in the castle. It has an oddly specific floral pattern with a waterfall in the background. The door is also made of a darker wooden material.

I hear noises on the other side. "What do you mean I'm the chosen one? I've never been chosen for anything except when everyone else was already picked. Are you sure you have the right person?"

Vanessa? What is she doing in there? I press my ear against the door to hear more. I know it is dishonest, but with the unorthodox ways she has been acting lately, I honestly do not know what her true feelings are. She also appears to be completely numb whenever I am around her.

"You'll do ANYTHING I want? Fine! Drain all of my emotions. Every single last one of them. I don't want to feel anything anymore."

"Wait. What? NO! Stop it!" Oh, I said that out loud. No point in hiding now. I barge in and try grabbing her, hoping it will stop her, but five bright-yellow rocks surround her and drain some sort of colorful entity from within Vanessa. Her eyes turn expressionless once more, and this time I think it is permanent. The rocks push me aside. "And now, I have another request, Starlight Prophecies. We will destroy the world I came from. First the living beings on it, then the planet itself."

"Vanessa, snap out of it! What has gotten into you?"

"Vanessa?" She tilts her head. "Who's that? My name is Neona."

"I do not care what you call yourself! You are just lost, dazed, and confused, just like me. But we can still be happy together, right?"

She grabs her staff and points it at me. "It seems you will jeopardize my plans. You will need to disappear."

"NO!" For some reason, my hair begins to spin. It spins so uncontrollably that it cuts the ground beneath me. When I get up, I move so fast that I break down castle doors and walls, until I find my brothers. My hair calms down. "Guys, we need to go back to Earth."

"What's the rush? We just got here. Besides, there's no way we can." Prismo holds up an ice-cold lemonade.

"You do not understand. Vanessa has gone mad. She wants to kill me. You guys are probably next."

"It's not April 1 yet. Can it with the ridiculous joke."

I grab Prismo by his shirt collar, forcing him to drop his lemonade. "Listen, you! I just lost my best friend to some rocks. They are giving her the power to annihilate everything she once knew. Either we get out of here and warn everyone, or we just die!" When I scream "die," my hair spins one more time. It cuts my skin. The pain is so intense, like the worst paper cut in your life magnified a hundredfold. I hunch over and grab the back of my neck, which is badly bleeding. Prismo finally believes me, gives me a towel for my neck, and we race to find the others.

In the room with the golf course, we find Rod. "Oh, hey, guys. Great day for a round of nine, right?"

"We're inside…" Nocturne points out.

"Not the focus here." I take deep breaths.

"You look like a cat just mauled you, Aria. Everything okay?" Rod squints.

"No. Everything is horrible. Vanessa is going to kill us all if we do not get out of here, now! She's lost her mind! OW!" I grasp the towel covering my wound harder than before. It's soaked. I feel dizzy… My brothers dive to catch me, but Rod catches first.

"What happened to her?" Rod looks at my brothers as if they did this to me.

"She cut herself with her hair," Prismo says. Rod squints again. He touches my hair to see if he is telling the truth.

"Oh, wow…" Rod's hands shake.

"What? What is it?" Nocturne gets up.

"Her hair is made of fine titanium. No wonder her wound is so deep. And from the looks of things, you two also have metal heads."

Chapter 24

More Prophecies, More Trouble
SIX YEARS AGO – ARIA

I am set down near a tree. Rod takes the towel attached to his golf bag and places it on my wound. He uses some sports tape to make sure it will not fall off.

"So where is Vanessa?" Rod asks.

"She was in a strange room with five floating yellow rocks. But that was a while ago. I have a feeling she is looking for us now," I answer.

"Floating yellow rocks?" Rod squints again. Why does he keep doing that? "It seems you've been through a lot. Just sit tight, and I'll look for her."

"That won't be necessary," a dead voice arises from behind the tree I am resting on. Rod flies to where it came from to protect me, but there is no one there. "Silly, I'm over here." The voice now comes from the putting green at the end of the first hole. "I'm in plain sight. Can't you see?"

Rod closes his eyes, his hair fluttering a bit. He opens them again, reaches into the tree, grabs Vanessa's heel, and flings her into the fairway. The five rocks follow her. After spitting the grass out of her mouth, she lifts her face. I can barely recognize it. Nothing about it looks like Vanessa. I guess she really is Neona now. Maybe if I call her that, it will make her happy? I do not know. It is worth a try.

"Stop this, Neona!" I call out with the remaining strength I have left. "You would not hurt a fly back on Earth."

"You are correct. I wouldn't. And what's my payment? Pain. And nothing but pain. All I know is pain. The chair I'm strapped in, the scientists around me, the liquids within the vaccines, and the electric shock. All of it. Nothing but pain. There is no salvation for a world like that. It's better off gone. And that is exactly what I will bring."

"You will be no better than the scientists who mutated you! Do you not see? They are already gone. Not everyone on Earth is mean to you. Look at me! Do you feel anything when you see me now?" My eyes water. Please say yes…

"Anything that isn't a part of my plan is just a reminder of my pain. So yes, I do feel something when I see you. And it's pain. I'll make sure you understand what I mean." She points her staff at me once again.

Rod ducks his shoulder and prepares to ram her. She looks at him and reveals a videotape. Rod stops. "What is that?"

"Your will. And it's mine. You wouldn't want anyone to see you killing all of these scientists with your powers, would you?" Neona slips it back into her pocket.

"No… NO!" He tries tackling her, but she teleports out of the way.

"Ah, ah, ah. That's not how my new commander acts. But since I'm in a festive mood today, I'll let it slide."

"Grr…"

"And as your new queen, I command you to kill the woman beneath the tree."

"Rod…?" I look at him. His eyes are beneath his bangs.

"I can't…"

"DO IT NOW, OR THE UNIVERSE WILL HAVE ACCESS TO THIS TAPE!" Neona's eyes come back to life.

"Forgive me, Aria." He tucks his shoulder and begins charging again. His stomps are loud. They are making the noises surface. CH… ChCHC…

"YES! KILL HER. DO IT NOW, SO MY PAIN WILL BE ALLEVIATED!"

"CHCHCHHCHCHZZZZZZZZZZZCHCHCHCHCZZZZZ! NO

SUCH THING WILL HAPPEN. YOU WILL NOT FEEL ANYTHING AFTER THIS, NEONA."

Kekekekekeke! They have consumed me! My hair is running wild! They fuel me with power. That is all I need right now. Power. And lots of it!

I slice the land Rod is running on and use my hair to punch him to the ceiling.

"Ohh, you seem to be hurting." She must be referring to my rustic-yellow glowing scar, shaking smile, and multi-ring layered eyes. It is nothing. The wound that once hurt me is now the source of my power. "Let me make the pain go away."

"Fool! I do not feel pain. I do not feel anything, except remorse for your shredded corpse." My hair whirls around, allowing me to fly. I slash at Neona, but she teleports away. She thrusts her staff forward, ordering her five rocks to charge at me. I reflect them all with the hurricane-force winds emanating from my hair. The rocks then form pillars of light and try to close me in. But I race out and slash at Neona, who clearly was not expecting me to move so fast. She escapes a fatal blow, but I shred her right arm. She barely notices. "Does it not hurt?"

"The pain I felt inside is far worse. This is like a paper cut." From behind, Neona's staff is sliced in half.

"That's enough, psycho." Nocturne's hair stops spinning.

"Now surrender here, or you're in for a world of pain."

"Hehehehe…   HAHHHHHAHAAHAHHAHAaaAAHHhhhAH! Starlight Prophecies, reset button, go!" The five rocks encircle all of us, and we are booted out of the castle.

Chapter 25

There Is No Escape
SIX YEARS AGO - NEONA

I could not risk dying. Not yet. I need to realize my plan to the best of my abilities. Then I can die.

– *Starlight Prophecies, are you all right?*

– *Yes, ma'am. We're at your service.*

– *Excellent. I wish to remodel the castle before those three reenter. First, fix my staff.*

– *Yes, ma'am.*

– *Thank you. Now, for the blueprints I desire.* I wave my staff, and my dream blueprints for the castle appear, along with a title on the top: "Castle Kusondela."

– *Right away, ma'am. We will get to work now.*

I leave them to their business, as I have a much-greater task at hand. I slam my staff into the ground of my bedroom, cracking it slightly. Using light as my eyes, I search the Milky Way Galaxy for the planet Mars, where the shipwreck and bodily remains still lie.

"Come on…! Just a little more. Show me the way!" I find the Sun, then Mercury, then Venus, then Earth, and, finally… "There's Mars. Now, to transport everything into the basement. Light, assist me."

I remove my staff from the ground, and all remains on Mars are neatly organized into piles in the basement. There is metal on one side, and the decaying bodies with their trapped souls on the other.

Now the souls will have nowhere to run. They will be my citizens, and the vessels of my power. The illusion I am preparing in this castle will trick anyone into thinking it never ends. It's foolproof.

"Rod, can you hear me?" Using the light, I project my voice throughout the castle.

"Ungh… yes?" He's still angry. It's so cute. Almost sad, but mostly cute.

"Go to the basement. Use the power I will provide you to give new life to the bodies there."

"The bodies…? What?"

"Do not question me."

"Yes, ma'am."

When Rod reaches the basement, he looks around like he's unsure of what he's supposed to do. He asks Neona what exactly she wants from him.

"See the syringe on the floor next to the bowl of tough orange liquid?"

"Yes, I do."

"Use that to suck up some of the orange liquid, and place a drop on each decaying head. It will be enough to revitalize them."

"Fine, but what exactly is this orange liquid?"

"Syrusima. It's called Syrusima. Once you're done, I'll tell you what to do with the metal."

Chapter 26

Passed On, But Not for Long
SIX YEARS AGO - ROD

This day sucked.

Not only can I not go home, but I also have to do some demented child's dirty work so she can destroy her home planet.

Seriously, think about it. I am taking half-decayed human bodies and revitalizing them using a syringe, the same tool that destroyed them. Can't I just let the spirits leave in peace? I'll die if that happens, though, because of that stupid tape. I need to find Nexus and bring him back first!

I load up the syringe with some of that Syrusima stuff that the queen provided me. Ugh… this smell. Have you ever been to a garbage dump when it's on fire? No? Well, that is what this basement smells like. I'm not sure what I feel worse for: my nose or the spirits of the bodies.

Regardless, I can't disobey the queen. She has a trump card over my head, which she can slam down at any time. Though I don't think she understands the scope of damage she will cause by revealing that tape.

"It's okay, young'un. I'll lighten your load a little bit."

"Who's there?" I squint, trying to sense the presence of someone new.

"Just me, laddie." Something is encircling the metal at blisteringly high speeds. Before I have the chance to even see what it is, it and the metal are gone!

"Queen! Someone just stole the metal. What do we do?"

"Don't fret, commander. I know what just happened. Leave that to me. We will get the metal back in due time."

"Yes, Queen!" Phew, I got off that one easy.

Now, back to reviving the dead. I push the end of the syringe so a drop of it falls onto the first half-scalp/half-skeleton I see. Upon contact, the liquid encloses the body like a cocoon.

"What… are you doing?" a frail voice calls out from within the cocoon.

"I'm not even sure myself…" I put my head down. This is a disgrace. With no choice but to continue, I encase every body in the room into a cocoon.

"Queen, I've done what you have asked of me. Now what?"

"Give it a day. The bodies should return to normal. It's then that we'll run a field test."

I don't like the sound of that at all.

"So, what is this field test you were mentioning?" I ask the queen.

"This." She pounds her staff, bringing one of the revitalized humans into her room. "Starlight Prophecies, front and center!" Her five slaves warp right to her. I can't imagine they want to do this either. "See if you can charge your power into this person." They line up in a pentagon formation and shoot tiny beams of light into the person's forehead. There is no reaction. "Hmm… try it again." Neona gently places the bottom of her staff onto the person's bare foot. The prophecies fire again. "As I feared."

"What is it?"

"Their souls are getting in the way of the power."

"Well, maybe so, but won't they need their souls to live?" I fear her response.

"That is my decision, not theirs."

What can I say at this point? Neona disgusts me. Where's Aria? Maybe she'll bring Vanessa back.

Chapter 27

Veniss' Invocation
SIX YEARS AGO - ARIA

"Ne-o-na! Let. Us. In!" I slash at the door with my hair, but nothing is happening to it.

"You're doing it all wrong, sisty." Nocturne confronts the door. He sticks his hands out at the door. "Open sesame!"

"Really? At a time like this, you really think that–" Wow, it actually opened.

"You were saying?" Nocturne puts his hands behind his back.

"Shut up." I run inside. The castle is totally different. There was never a foyer this big before. Also, I do not remember there only being two sets of stairs in the first room.

And I certainly do not remember Neon unconscious on the floor. I skid on my knees to his aid. "Neon? You okay?" I slap his face, gently of course.

"Uh... huh? Neon? Who's Neon? I'm Veniss."

"NO! Snap out of it." I slap him across the face harder this time.

"Uhehehe. Calm down, dudette. Everything's all right."

"How can you say that? You just lost your memory!"

"I did? Nah, you must be trippin'. Anywho, I'm gonna go find my sis. She said something about you guys too. So, come on up." He is so relaxed all of a sudden. Neona must have done this to him. I am sure of it. It is just a way of silencing Neon, so she can destroy Earth without resistance.

"Okay. We'll catch up soon." I wave to him.

Veniss walks up the left staircase.

"Oh, dear. I'm afraid that's not an option." Neona's voice fills the room.

"Show yourself. I'll tear you to shreds and bring Vanessa back!" My hair gets violent.

"So sorry, but you won't get the chance." A rocket materializes out of nowhere and encases the three of us.

"Hey! What is this?" I slash at the walls, but they're covered in some tough orange liquid.

"Your imprisonment. Goodbye." The foyer floor parts, and we are launched into the deep recesses of space. "And now my brother's shattered spirit will consume them." Neona whispers.

"No! Come on! BREAK!" I can barely dent this thing. "Do not just sit there, be useful and help me break this rocket open."

"Okay, bossy." My brothers finally join in, but to no avail. Nothing is happening. In fact, parts of our hair keep getting stuck.

"Hey, look, we're approaching some planet." Prismo can barely decipher what is outside the pod window because of the goop.

"Is that Mars? It looks red."

"Do you know how many planets there are in the universe? That can be anything. I doubt Neona would send us back to the planet where we can stop her plan."

"Sadly, she's right, Nocturne." Prismo looks down.

"Come on, guys! Look at the bright side–"

"Listen, you! There IS no bright side here." I grab Nocturne's shirt collar. "I just lost my best friend to some rocks, the only help we had is trying to kill us, and now we are in untamed space. What possible bright side could there be?"

"Terminal velocity?" Prismo looks at us as he points outside. We are approaching this red planet's atmosphere, which means there is no stopping our impact if we cannot break this rocket soon. How are we going to do that if we have not been able to this entire trip? Our lives depend on it, though.

"Come on! Spin! Spin your hair like the wind!" The surrounding air gets louder as our velocity increases. You can barely hear our hair spinning with all the flames outside the vessel. "Break, you stupid goo!" Nocturne and Prismo look at each other, nod, and surround me. "What are you idiots doing? Spin your blades!" They move in closer. I don't want to hurt them, so I stop spinning.

"Go back!"

"No. You're our only hope." Prismo hugs me.

No... they know I cannot cut the goo. They are sacrificing themselves so I can live! No... please. No more. My mind cannot handle losing you two.

"You'll be able to stop Neona. She was once your best friend. If anyone will bring her back, it's you, Aria." Nocturne hugs my other side.

"No! Stop it! We will get through it together. You guys are all I have left..."

Splat. The rocket crashes. Five dark yellow rocks fly out of the cockpit.

Chapter 28

The Alpha Extinction
SIX YEARS AGO – NEONA

We have now landed on Arsm. It seems I will not only be able to dispose of the souls I do not need, but also be able to check on the three I disposed of. In case they need any more… guidance. "Are you ready, commander?"

"Yes. Let the purification begin."

"Excellent. Move it, people, let's go!" The humans come out one by one, shackled together. "We're taking a stroll up the mountain today."

They all mumble. It's not like they'll be able to feel anything after this, so I don't care.

"Ahhhhhhhh! My leg! MY LEEEEEEEEG!" One of the boys near the front breaks his leg, completely snapping it. I go to have a look. "Aww, you're hurt. A shame. I forgot my medical kit back home. Sooooorry." I leave him be. The chains will drag him along. He won't fall behind. "Well? What are you all waiting for? Jump into the well." Everyone, in a puny act of defiance, sits down. "All of you are hurt? Jeez, the things I do for you guys. You better thank me later." I pound my staff on the floor. A wave of light lifts all of them high into the air and drops them on the top of the mountain. There, a deep, deep well waits, but there is no water in it. The chain drags all of them in.

SPLAT.

SPLAT.

SPLAT.

Splat.

Splat.

Splat.

Splat.

Splat.

Splat.

Splat. Splat. Splat... splat... silence.

Good. That's all of them.

"Finally we are free... AND YOU ARE IN OUR DOMAIN, NEO-NA. You will experience the pain you made all of us feel."

I notice that the planet is covered in scrap metal. "Too late. Nothing you do will worsen my p-p---p-pain." Whoa. My entire head just twitched. At any rate, with the light's guidance, I combine the power of light with the scrap metal to make a tsunami. It crashes on all of the souls trying to escape the mountain and encases them inside. "And now, for your bodies." I lift my staff high into the air and exhume the bodies from the mountain. I check to make sure Rod is still behind me. Good. He's starting to become more obedient. That's one less soul for me to deal with. "I will leave you all here now. You are free to do what you want."

"That's... not fair," I hear a defeated voice from the bottom of the hole.

"You've trapped us inside the scrap. Let us go! We've done nothing to you."

"Thank you for understanding. I was afraid I'd have to do some horrible things to get you to cooperate." I encase all of the bodies in a massive obsidian safe.

I hear the sounds of a hurricane and cracking thunder. "CHCH-CHHCHCHZZZZZZZZZZCHCHCHCHCZZZZZ!"

"Ah... Aria. It's good to see you've embraced the light's guidance. Good girl." She looks just like when I last saw her. Except this time, she's not killing me. Excellent. The Vanity Prophecies have done their job.

"CHCHHhhHH!"

"Behave now, okay? I'll be sure to let you know when my wondrous plan succeeds."

"I'll… stop you."

I bop her head with the back end of my staff, knocking her out.

"Come, commander. We must leave. The bodies are secured. But first…" I throw a bottle of Syrusima into the sky. With a pillar of light from my staff, it explodes, releasing the liquid into the atmosphere. With the light's assistance, I cover the atmosphere in Syrusima. It hardens, and closes the planet off. No one else gets in, and no one else gets out. "There. Now we can leave."

With the wave of my staff, we are back at the Space Garden. Time to create my soulless army of prophecy-powered mutants.

Chapter 29

Soul-powered Mechazilla

How can this be real? Neona? Tormenting the souls of thousands? She seemed so wise and protective of her people when we first met her, but... I'm not sure what to feel right now.

Griff has his entire right hand over his face.

Azilez suppresses the urge to vomit.

Vizor's legs can't stop quivering.

Z and D are hugging.

"What the hell did we just see?" I hold my head with both hands, barely able to comprehend it. "I refuse to believe what I just saw was real."

"I'm... not sure." Griff grasps his head tighter.

"I don't understand how the prophecies, the shining example of essence and valiance, can be used to trap and torture the souls of that many people."

– It must be frustrating. I must say, I can't exactly understand how you feel, but try not to let these wicked thoughts control your mind. Look where it got Neona.

– Grr...!

– V, calm down! Your evil form will surface otherwise. Remember what happened last time? Griff and Azilez were nearly killed.

"Just because she has power... she thinks she can push everyone around. It's not fair." My eyes exude white mist. Z and D fly next to me and try to snap me out of my little fit, but this injustice can't go unpunished! I can't believe we supported her in the Phantom Pipeline invasion. Griff was right. There is something going on here. Something big. How could I have been so naive?

"Ergh… huh? Where am I? Where is Vanessa?" Aria's bronze eyes glisten with the stars in the sky.

"V! Neona didn't bend everyone to her will. Look! There's still one person she tried to kill that's still here." Azilez points at Aria.

"WhO goEs tHErE?" Voices become audible from the surrounding scrap metal.

"EVIL V." My eyes nearly go blank.

"V, stop it!" D comes in from behind and hugs me. "If you give in to your powers, you won't be any better than that mean girl in the memories!"

GRRR! I should calm down. D's right. But I don't know what to do. I just want to vent. My evil form feels like it wants to punch through a wall.

"Distraction!" Azilez yells.

"HUH?" Her hand flies across my face. OOF, I immediately revert to normal. "Uhh… thanks for that."

"Anytime!" She winks. Her stomach seems to be under control.

"TypICaL. AlWaYs ignorEd foR soMeThiNG 'morE important.'" That voice sounds like it's been drinking acid instead of water.

"We've got to get out of here. There are thousands of spirits here, lusting for vengeance." Vizor can sense them inside the scraps. He jets in the opposite direction.

"Where would we go, though?" I chase him.

"Away from here, for sure."

"ToO laTe." The metal scraps surround us. "ThoSe YelLoW rOckS haVe cAuSeD us mUCh PaiN."

"YOu sEEm tO hAve roCks jUSt likE tHe onEs NeONa haD."

"WhiCH iS whY We won'T leT yOu LEavE unTiL ThEy'Re ouRs." The individual rusty scraps begin combining. KLING. KLANG. CHING. CHANG. A plate of chest armor forms. Then a left arm. Then a massive drill for the right arm. Then two legs. And, finally, an angry face with glowing, red eyes.

"CoMe HERe, liTTLe RocKiEs." The mechazilla grabs at the ten prophecies. Griff uppercuts the left arm to parry it.

"We're never losing the prophecies again. Especially to a bunch who'll just abuse their powers." Griff assumes a fighting stance, fists clenched and feet shoulder-width apart.

"Got that right!" Vizor instantly stuffs the Solar Prophecies into Griff's backpack and the Shadow Prophecies into his hair blades.

"yOu'LL sTiLL bE bEAten tO a PulP."

All of us explode into our chaos forms and charge. The mechazilla fires off its mighty drill, rushing into a tree that D sprang up. The forces of the two cancel out and they disappear. The spirit machine grows another drill. I guess it would've been a little easy otherwise. We've got to find a way to disable that drill.

"How's this?" Vizor straps on his grappling hook onto the ends of his hair blades. He tosses one end around the bot and grabs it as it comes around. As the bot eyes him, he continuously spins around, gaining momentum.

Azilez takes the opportunity to assist him. With the wave of her chaos form's staff, she creates a gigantic blue-white-red Popsicle. "Vizor! Throw 'em here!"

"If you say so." Vizor loosens his grip, and the bot spins toward Azilez.

"Hey, fellas! Ever heard of a bomb pop?"

"Uh oh." She throws down the frozen treat. KABLOOEY! The bits of the bot scatter everywhere and the drill disappears.

"Now's our chance, Z! Griff! Let's charge it." Before we can even manage to, the bot is back in one piece, and it grows a new drill.

"NiCe FiREwoRkS." The bot fires off three drills at once this time. I dodge the first two but the last one gets me. Even so, the second it contacts me it disintegrates. I am barely scathed.

"Ohh. That might work too," I murmur to myself. "Azilez! Some pizza dough sounds lovely right about now."

"Coming right up!" She waves her staff and flings the ball of uncooked dough at the bot. It launches a drill at the dough and jumps away.

"Now!" I fire off a white-hot fireball, which the bot dodges. Though I never planned to hit it.

"FORE!" Z swings at the fireball with a full-force driver, sending it back to the bot at a blistering speed. With zero time to react, all of the metal on the bot combusts, setting the spirits free from their metal scraps.

"Yes! Finally!" Hey, their voices sound normal now.

"We've been set free!"

"It's what we've wanted for years. Our suffering has finally ended."

"Wait. I thought you guys wanted the prophecies." I twirl my hair.

"We don't want anything to do with Neona's or your rocks, who-ever you are. We're finally going to leave this horrid galaxy and find new horizons. Goodbye, forever!" All of the spirits disperse.

"Huh. That was… strange."

"What? They're happy we set them free." Griff flies closer to me.

"No, I get that, but how did they just completely flip their convic-tions like that? I thought they were really after the prophecies."

"That's not fair to say at all."

I sense a powerful presence behind me.

Chapter 30
The King's Return

It's Neon! Well, not physically. His body is back on the Space Garden. But his spirit's here, right in front of us. He looks just like he does on the Space Garden, except his entire body, including his clothes, is yellow.

"Neon, is that really you?" I'm relieved to see he's in one piece.

"How do you know who I am?" He becomes defensive all of a sudden.

"Hey, that is not a nice way to thank someone who just set you free!" Aria flies up to him, using her hair as a propeller.

"Stay away from them. How do you know they're on our side? They have those same rocks that Neona has."

"Stop calling her that! You know that is not her name. Besides, not all rocks are untrustworthy. You were trapped inside those five dark-yellow-colored rocks for a long time yourself, possessing me! And I still trust you. You would not possess me like that willingly," Aria argues.

"That's not the point here! Answer me or I'll smash them!" Okayyyyy, dude. I'd like to see you try.

"They just fought and freed me from my insanity."

"You'll never be freed of that, and you know it too! Stop lying to yourself."

"What is your problem, Neon?" Aria clutches the bottom of her throat, half-insulted.

"I just don't trust anyone with those rocks! And you shouldn't either. Neo... I mean, Vanessa controlled your mind with them for years." Neon points at Griff's backpack.

"Hey! Feeling's mutual, bub!" Speedy shouts from inside the bag.

"Can it," Griff orders.

"It's not her fault! She just…"

"Stop defending her. She brought the dead back to life, only to kill them again and trap their spirits to fulfill her desires. Tell me, whose fault was that?"

"…"

"As I thought."

"Hey, look, Neon–" I try to intervene.

"Don't talk to me like you understand. I don't care that you just set a thousand spirits free. I have no idea what your intentions are."

"Don't hate us just because of the prophecies."

"So that's what they're called…" Neon pounds his right fist into his left palm. "In that case, I'll crush them! And you next."

"Stop it!" Aria's hurricane hair blows all of us away. "Neon, I will not let you fight them. They have earned my trust."

"Why? Why do you trust them? Those prophecies have ruined our lives."

"Yes, and they also just put it back on track. V, Z, D, Griff, Vizor, and Azilez just taught me that the prophecies' powers could be controlled. Please, Neon, we do not have much time. Vanessa could destroy the Earth soon!"

"Hmph! Fine. I won't like it, though. I still don't trust them. But I do trust you, Aria." Neon pouts, crosses his arms, and slouches.

"Oh, thank you! It is good to have you back."

"Well, it's great that we got Neon's spirit back, but we still have no idea where we are," Z points out.

"Then let's find out." Vizor scrambles in the vicinity, frantically searching for a sign of anything familiar. We all follow his example. Since we're still unsure whether Neon will cooperate with us or not, we stay in our chaos forms.

"Hey, guys! I found something," Z hollers.

"Really? What is it?" I rush to his side.

"This asteroid." He points to a floating space rock I've never seen before.

"Ah. And what's so special about this asteroid?"

"It's in outer space."

"And…?"

"That's all I got."

"Unbelievable." You can always count on Z to get you out of a pinch.

"Aha! This is a good indication of where we are," Vizor calls out. Hopefully this'll go better than Z's attempt. "What is it, Vizor?"

"See for yourself."

I spot a blue planet, about the size of Earth. It has blades for rings, much like the blades in Vizor's hair. I know only one planet that has those distinct rings. "Treah!"

"That's right. We're in my home turf, Crystal Fog Galaxy. We must be on Arsm, since it is the closest neighbor to my home planet. I could lead the way back to the Space Garden. Ready everyone?" We nod in agreement, except Neon. He just turns to Aria, looking worried. "Good. Let's move out!"

Chapter 31

Beetle Beat Down

It's exhilarating to finally fly at my true speed. Ever since slogging through the ocean to get to Washington, DC, I've been itching to go fast! We arrive back at the Space Garden in no time at all. Despite the fact that there was a battle going on when we were forced to leave, nothing has changed.

"I don't like this. It's too quiet here." Vizor looks around, swaying his head left and right.

– *Can someone hear me?* A frail feminine voice calls out.

– *What was that?* I almost jump from the break in silence.

– *I'm not sure, but it seems to be coming from the castle's peak.* The Dark Spirit points from within me.

– *Hold it. I recognize that voice. Orient? Is that you?* Neon can sense spirits too? I mean, considering he IS a spirit, it makes sense. I wonder... can all spirits sense other spirits?

– *Neon? Where have you been? You've been doing a horrible job keeping an eye on my granddaughter!*

– *Err... yeah, that's Orient. Cranky as ever, I see. Where are you?*

– *Where do you thin-kkkff?* It sounds like Orient's false teeth just flew out of her mouth.

– *Just making sure.* Neon eases his uptight shoulders. The familiar voice must have soothed him. "Orient is calling out to us from the castle top. She needs our help!"

"Vanessa's grandma? But she died, right?" Azilez rests her head on her staff.

124

"We actually don't know that. We just never saw her after 'that' incident. She could be alive. Look at Aria and Vanessa. They survived the experiments."

We soar to the top of the castle, but after going through the glass window, we end up back at the gates. Well, sort of.

See, there's an entrance here, but nothing else. Everything around us just disappeared. It's all white space.

"Vanessa is up to her antics again." Aria holds her hands to the bottom of her throat.

"Don't worry. We'll get her back." I hate seeing a troubled face. Neon glares at me. I pretend not to notice.

Expecting utter hell, I pull the castle doors open and everyone walks inside. To my surprise, we arrive in a school field similar to the one we saw in the beginning of Aria's memories. Mud pits fill the sides and corners, while the center is overflowing with untrimmed grass. Like the entrance, there's only a field here. Everything else is white space.

"I thought you wanted to stay away from Earth, Vanessa. Do you finally miss it?" Aria shouts to the blue sky above. A grotesque, giant albino beetle drops down. Its front pinchers chomp.

"SSSSHHHHRRRRAAAA!"

"Bring it on! I've fought bigger." Vizor draws his hair blades.

This isn't sitting well with me. I doubt Vanessa would throw a single, giant beetle at us with no other tricks up her sleeve. I'll stay away from it for now. Can you blame me? Merely touching the castle sent us here.

I take to the skies and begin my volley of fireballs to see how the creature will avoid them. It just sits there, but a pile of mud flies in the way, tanking my blasts. As I look back to the ground, I see hundreds and hundreds of moving mud piles, trying to get my friends stuck. Z and D fly to try and avoid them, but those little critters can jump rather high. Just great.

"Get back, heathens!" D continuously slashes at a bunch of mud piles, but they shrug it off. He then summons a gun made of mahogany wood. "Try this on for size." D pulls the trigger, and covers the mud piles in tree sap. It doesn't mix well with them. "It's working! Vizor, make like a sprinkler and spin around." D shoots at Vizor's hair blades, drenching them in sap.

"You owe me new blades."

"Azilez, shield us. That sap will take forever to get out if it gets in your hair."

"RIGHT AWAY!" Azilez, grabbing her hair with her free hand, arcs her staff, and a rainbow encases everyone, except Vizor, who pivots and spins. The sap is thrown everywhere, destroying all of those little mud piles. The big beetle is not fazed by it.

"SSSSSHHHHHHRRRRAAAA!" It jumps into the white space and disappears.

"Did it just give up?" I ask.

"No. It's hiding in the light – a common trick Vanessa uses to get the jump on someone or something." Neon's legs transform into bursts of light. He scatters across the field, trying to sense where the beetle might be. "V! Three o'clock."

I throw a fireball at the emptiness.

"SSSSSHHHAAAA!" The beetle flings out of the wall, waving its claws.

"Now's our chance." Neon, fist first, rockets right through the beetle, frying its wings.

Aria slices and dices it with her hair until there's nothing left.

The field disappears, and we're dropped into Star Security's headquarters. There's no one here either.

Chapter 32

Renegade Rod

"**S**eems like we finally made it into the actual castle." I gaze at the mother computer.

"Don't think you're in the home stretch just yet." The silver-haired Commander Rod walks out from behind an employee's desk. "I can't let you pass."

"Sure you can," Aria says. "But you choose not to."

He squints at her. "Trust me when I say I don't want to do this. But I have no choice."

"We don't need a sob story right now, Rod. Our target's the queen."

"Then my target is you. None shall pass." He quakes the ground while stomping toward us. Computers fall down, one by one. His stride steadily increases until it becomes a full-on sprint. Rod carries that momentum into a flip dive. We scatter, and he destroys the railing above.

"Hrgh!" Griff blasts his hair onto Rod, who reflects it back at him with his bare arms.

"It'll take a lot more than that to topple me." Rod knees Griff in the gut, sending him into the mother computer.

Azilez flips her staff, and rainbow waves splash out of the hole in the mother computer. Instead of drowning in them, Rod swims to Azilez and delivers a roundhouse that knocks the wind out of her.

Vizor takes his multi-flame-covered hair blades and swings at Rod. He tries a quick stab, but Rod fades back and goes in for a punch. Vizor parries and dents Rod on the head with his right blade's handle.

"Oof! Hrrrrrrrah!" Rod grabs Vizor's blades out of his hands and throws them on him.

– *Dark Spirit, help them out!* I call to It.

– *Right away.*

It rushes out of my body and bolts at them.

– *Good. That should take a minute or two.*

"What's the matter, V? Surprised that I tore through your friends' powers so easily?"

"Honestly, I'm more surprised that you haven't found a way to knock that tape out of Vanessa's hands." I know I should be scared of Rod right now, but I'm not. I have no idea how he gets that insane power, but still.

"She works with the light. There's nothing more absolute-ch-hzzzzzzchhchczz- than the light."

Aria falls to her knees and grasps the ground.

"What the...? A hologram?"

BLeeeeeEEEeeeEPpp... Rod disappears into thin air. Another door appears on top of the mother computer's remains.

"Dark Spirit, how are Griff, Vizor, and Azilez?"

"Like you need to ask!" Griff pats my shoulder from behind. "I'm revved up and ready to go."

"Same here." Vizor picks up his blades from the floor. They light with flames once they touch his own head.

"I'm all good, too!" Azilez dusts her dress off with her staff. Her hair is somehow fine after all that. I doubt tree sap would've done anything to it.

"Aria!" Neon holds her shoulders tight. "Snap out of it. C'mon, we don't have time for this, and you know it."

"Were you not the one who said..." Her hair covers her face. "I SHOULD EMBRACE THIS?" The force of her hair hurricane-sweeps Neon off his knees. "Come on, Neon. Let us not keep Vanessa waiting any longer." Aria's voice reverts to normal, and even her smile is under control. She's beginning to control her psychotic self!

Chapter 33

Monarch's Madness

Aria opens the door, and all of us barge in. We're somehow in the queen's chamber, at the top of the castle. Can I really say that, though? Look how much bigger this room has become! I'd wager it's the size of two football fields.

Even more unsettling, the entire Space Garden population is poised in military lines in front of Vanessa. I can't see any of their irises, and their body languages are all the same. It's like they're robots and Vanessa has the remote that controls them all.

"Oh, hello, everyone!" Vanessa seems too excited to see us. She sits on her throne, back upright and staff in hand, with the Phantom Reactor behind her. "Do not fret. The menaces have been dealt with. And it seems you're safe too. Excellent."

"Don't act like you're happy to see us, Vanessa." Neon's spirit throws his arms in frustration. "Your guests know everything we do."

"They do?" She doesn't sound particularly frightened or upset about that. In fact, her tone hasn't changed at all. "Oh, well. I guess you should meet them now. It won't change anything." Five bright-yellow tablets appear from behind the throne.

Griff holds his hands to his head, shaking. Vizor's eyes water, but he never sheds a tear. His eyebrows drop.

– *AGH! It hurts!* I grab my stomach.

– *Don't worry, V. It's just noise.*

"Oh, you can hear them too? Wow, impressive." Vanessa applauds us. The entire room claps with her. So much noise… so much noise… SO

MUCH NOISE!

"Enough!" Neon flings his arm in the air, sending a light-induced shockwave straight at the prophecies. "This doesn't involve them. Not everyone needs to feel pain like we did. Aria and I see that. Why can't you?"

Vanessa lets out a hearty laugh, like Neon just told a good joke. "You're mistaken. I'm fine. Look at me. I've done so much. Created a whole race of mutants, stopped the Phantom Pipeline's advancement into my territory, and created a miracle orange dietary supplement that replaces the need for any food or water. How can I be in pain?"

"Yo, sis! Who's that freaky floatin' dude over there yellin' at you?" Veniss, Neon's host body, plops up from the floor beside the throne.

"You...!" Neon clenches his fist. "What have you done to me?"

"What are you talking about, Neon? This is how you always act, you goofball." Vanessa crosses her arms, disappointed in her brother.

"It... it's done." A dilapidated Unknown Phantom falls to the ground from behind the Phantom Reactor.

"Good job. Now we can begin. Neon, enter the reactor, if you please." For a second, Vanessa's smile and head vibrate while her left eye twitches.

"No way I'm going near you."

"Are you sure?" Neon's spirit begins to move. None of us know how, but it ends up right next to Vanessa, who uses the back of her staff to push Neon into Veniss, making them one again. "Rod, if you would open the lid on the top."

"Yes, ma'am." He jumps onto the black machine from behind. Using both hands, he pops open the lid like a cork.

"In you go now, Neon. The purification of Earth depends on you." Bzzzzzzzzzzzz! "Mrrrfff!"

Aria's hair cuts across Vanessa's face. Aria rushes to Neon's side. "Not this time, dear friend."

"This is how you repay me? After all I've given you two?" She removes her free hand from her face, revealing a blood-red gash cutting straight across.

"Doesn't that hurt? At all?" Neon clenches his fists.

"This scratch?… No. It's just how I smile." Vanessa fires a blinding light at both of them. Vizor throws his ignited hair blades in the way and redirects the blast into Rod, rendering him unconscious. "Huh." Vanessa is hardly fazed by the fact that her commander might be dead. She keeps firing away at the three of them.

I rocket at Vanessa. Griff, Azilez, D, and Z are behind me. She teleports, and we crash into the reactor. It barely dents.

"That's a tough hunk of metal." I shake my head, readjusting my balance. "Where'd she go?" The entire room changes again. Now there is an endless sea of citizens surrounding us, with nothing else in sight. "Stop hiding behind your powers!" I shake my fist in the air, knowing Vanessa is watching.

– *Wait a second! Your powers. V, that's it!*

– *Huh?* It seems like the Dark Spirit just had a revelation.

– *Look around the citizens' feet. Do you notice anything?*

– *They're all wearing the same shoes?*

– *Okay, besides that.*

I look again. I don't see anything else worth noticing. …Wait a second. That's the problem! There's something absent that should be there.

– *Oh, yeah! Their shadows are missing.*

– *Yes! Vanessa can only hide behind the light because it has no contrast. Go on, let's mix my powers with yours and burst into your pure chaos form.*

Concentrating on the powers of the Solar Prophecies, Shadow Prophecies, the Dark Spirit, and, most of all, myself, Pure Chaos V enters the arena. My feet now emanate dark energy, in addition to the seizure-inducing hair, misty mitts, and scarlet-red eye of my chaos form. The infinite illusion fades away, revealing the queen's room once more.

"Enough tricks, Vanessa." The Dark Spirit's voice and mine combine, like during Dark V's transformation.

"W-w--w----what?" Her voice glitches.

"Light without darkness cannot exist, and darkness without light cannot exist. There is no world of only light, and there is no world of only darkness. The two exist with each other in balance. And that balance will never be broken, no matter how hard you try."

"H---ehe---heehehe-he----hehe. That's cool! Where can I get black lighting effects like that?" Vanessa doesn't seem to care for my comments at all.

– *V, it's no use. Nothing will get through to her at this point.*

– *No. Everyone has a tipping point. We just need to find Vanessa's. No one is ever a lost cause.*

"Rod, deal with them please while I deal with my brother."

"Yes, ma'am. Of course." Rod jumps down from the reactor and makes the ground quake, shattering it.

"Is your secret *that* worth it? You realize she'll destroy the entire Earth if she goes through with this, right? And left unchecked, she'll continue to destroy more." Silence. It's like Rod's under a spell. "You disgust me." I charge him with my new pure-chaos transformation, but bounce off him like a rubber ball. Next time I charge, I go for the queen, but he moves faster and blocks me. Everyone tries charging at the queen at once, and he still finds time to not only block all of us, but roundhouse us too.

"The queen is absolute." He crosses his arms.

"Very good, Rod."

If Rod is this powerful, why is he working for anyone? He can easily squash the queen. I need to get that tape from her!

"Now you must go into the reactor with my Starlight Prophecies, Neon. It'll be fun. Trust me."

"Trust you? Never again." He tries pummeling her using his lower torso rocket, but she merely teleports out of the way.

"Come on, pleeeeease?" She claps her bloody hand and her other hand together. At this point, there is so much blood on her face that it drips down onto the floor.

"Never!" He tries again. The same result.

"Know how it feels yet?" Vanessa teleports. He tries again. "Chasing something out of your reach?" Again. "Well, don't worry. The light will lead you there every time."

"No! It's all an illusion. An illusion that still has you fooled!" Again.

"Well, tell me something then. Is this an illusion?" Her eyes pop and she fires a white blast at Neon so powerful that the surrounding air oscillates. Neon tanks it pretty well initially, dispelling all of the excess light through his tail rocket. After a while, he can't hold on much longer, and he's caught inside a sphere, which Vanessa can control. She waves her staff and gently places it inside the Phantom Reactor. The Starlight Prophecies then rush inside, and Vanessa uses the same technique to close the reactor's lid. The light bubble pops and Neon is revealed, unconscious.

"Vanessa, no! STOP!" Aria tries rushing one last time, but Rod blocks her again.

"The queen is absolute."

"GET. OUT. OF. THE. WAY!" She punches him with her hair, but nothing happens. Each consecutive punch has less oomph in it. Aria's eyes droop further and further. Her face looks mentally excruciated. She falls over.

– Dark Spirit... help her. Please.

– I'll... try. It leaves my body and fills hers.

– Huh? What's... happening? Who are You?

– The Dark Spirit... I'm the Dark Spirit. V sent me to help you.

– O... K. THUD!

– Aria? Aria! Oh, no, she's out cold. The Dark Spirit rushes through her body, making sure all of her vital organs are functioning normally. With time, they are, but she still won't wake up. – It can't be too late yet. It can't be!

"And now to grind the ingredients together." Vanessa shoots the Phantom Reactor's switch on, and... ohhhh. I can't look. All I hear is CRACK! SNAP! POP! The light from the Starlight Prophecies is mixing with the Vanity Prophecies, or, in other words, with Neon himself.

"Neon... I'm sorry. I couldn't stop her." The Unknown Phantom tries touching the reactor, but faints first.

I'm the only conscious one left.

"And now time for the Omega Extinction." The reactor finishes mixing, and the Starlight Prophecies plop out. No sign of Neon. Not even his spirit. A metal cage encases all of the citizens in the room, who are still standing completely still. A tube connects from the top of the reactor to the top of the cage. The energy shoots out of the reactor and into the soulless bodies. When the cage is lifted, all of the citizens are revealed, now with bulbous yellow eyes and chaos powers. "Now, V. I'm afraid you'll have to leave." Vanessa thrusts her staff forward, signaling the citizens to trample me. The blood on Vanessa's face now stains all her clothes.

NO WAY AM I LETTING IT END LIKE THIS! "YYAAAAAAAAAAAAAAAAAAAAAAHHHHHHHHHHHHHHH!"

– *Oh, dear. This might be explosive.* The Dark Spirit rushes to place protective dark spheres around my friends.

The Starlight Prophecies, Vanity Prophecies, Shadow Prophecies, and Solar Prophecies' energies bombard around inside me. Four sets of prophecies, twenty tablets, and one spirit commanding it all with one goal in mind: STOP VANESSA!

My hair forms a giant "V" shape. My entire body ignites red flames, and my eyes become silver. I grow dragon wings that span about ten feet. On each pointed end, there is a dark orb that spews out black holes. Upon transformation, the entire Space Garden explodes.

DIVINE V!

Chapter 34

Power that Transcends the Speed of Light

"Wow, look at you, V. All of this power really suits you... because you just destroyed everything I worked for these past few years, you monster." Vanessa is still smiling, blood still spilling.

"You have no right to call anyone that," I respond, arms crossed.

"Again, it's not like it matters. Even if you have the powers of four sets of prophecies, how will you match thousands and thousands of chaos-powered beings by yourself?" She thrusts her staff forward again.

I open up one of the black orbs on my right wing, and a black hole forces all of the citizens to bonk heads.

She swipes her staff once from left to right, causing her entire army and her to teleport. ... As if it matters anymore.

"NO MORE HIDING!" I spiral out another black hole and it negates her attempt to teleport to Earth. They all are spit out in front of me. "If you want to get to Earth, you get past me first."

"V--v-v-v---v-v-v--er----yyyy-y well." Vanessa's face and voice glitch again. "Rod, you know what to do."

"Yes, ma'am!"

– *Dark Spirit? How much longer until they're all revived?*

– *A few minutes. Do you think you can hold them off for that long?*

– *Affirmative. Don't worry about me.*

– *Of course, chosen one!*

Rod jump-dives at me. I send him back to the queen with a swipe of my new wings. He tries getting behind me. I deny him every opportunity. The queen tries teleporting past me with her army. I spew out black holes to stop her. It's like I can see where they're going before they get there.

"I'm getting a sense of déjà vu here. Except there's less 'the queen is absolute.'"

"Grr!" Rod rolls up his jacket sleeves and lets out a flurry of punches. I enclose myself in my wings, blocking all of them. Growing bored, I flap my wings once and send everyone in front of me tumbling backward.

– *Done.*

– *Good job, Dark Spirit!*

– *Well, except for Aria. She is still showing no sign of waking up at all. Though I can feel her pulse beating.*

– *That's good. Just keep at it.*

"Wow, V! What happened to you?" Vizor rushes next to me from behind.

"All 20 prophecies."

"You combined all of them? Genius!"

"Maybe not." I look down.

"Why?" Vizor scratches his fiery blades.

"Hate to break up the chit-chat, but we've got company!" Griff launches forward with his rocket hair. He has a giant redwood in his arms.

"Round them up, Griff. They'll never find their way out of that!" D shakes his pendulum, almost dropping it.

Griff rams into as many chaos mutants he can, dwindling Vanessa's army.

"Hey, Z! Smack at this." Azilez sends a layer of chocolate sponge cake at him.

"Wait, what? …Whoa!" Z quickly whips out a five iron and whacks at it, hitting five chaos mutants.

"Again!" This time, vanilla. Then strawberry. Then lemon. Hazelnut. Coffee. Banana. And, finally, ginger spice. Because of Z's precise aim, all of the layers stack on top of each other. "Thanks for the confetti cake. Now to eat it!" Azilez materializes a rainbow hammer at the tip of her staff and slugs at it. Bits of the different cakes fly everywhere. I open my mouth to get some. ...Ew, I got coffee.

"Rod, where are you? You're supposed to be fighting V." Vanessa jerks her head in different directions.

"Queeeeeen, heeeeelp!" Rod calls from inside the bushels of leaves on the redwood.

"Well, that's annoying. I guess if you want something done right, you do it yourself!" Vanessa confronts me. "Fine. If it's no tricks you want, it's no tricks you'll get." She winds up her staff. I fly head-first at her. But something passes by and she's gone.

"ChhchcCHChchCzZZz!"

"Get... off of me!"

"CHCHCHZZZ!" Aria's back! But she can't control her powers this time.

– *Well, I'm not sure how that happened.* The Dark Spirit slides back into my body.

– *What do You mean?*

– *I tried everything. I made sure all of her vital signs were functioning at 100%, but nothing seemed to wake Aria up. Then, when I was about to leave, she just sprung to life and made a mad dash for Vanessa.*

– *Heh...* I try saying "huh," but my stunted breathing doesn't let me.

– *V? What's wrong?*

– *It's this divine form. It's... draining all of my energy.*

– *Not a problem! I'm here to help.* The Dark Spirit continuously loops through my body. – *I'll make sure you stay in peak condition.*

– *Thanks, Buddy.* My breathing reverts to normal. – *Now to nail Vanessa!*

When I find her again, Aria is hot on her tail, slashing at everything in sight. Vanessa fires a light sphere at her. Aria slices it in half. Vanessa flies under. Aria catches her with her quivering hands. She headbutts her. Vanessa's mouth wound tears further. Aria whips at her. Vanessa teleports out of Aria's grasp. That seems about all Vanessa can do: stall. We need to tire her out.

Or I can just trap her in a black hole. That'll work. But Aria is not letting up. It doesn't seem I can reason with her either. I don't want to risk trapping her too. I'll just use my fire and wings for now.

"CHchchCHCHZzz..." Aria's hair spirals faster.

"Ha!" Vanessa fires more pillars. Aria flies under them. She tries cutting Vanessa's feet, but she misses by literally a hair. "I've got to break that tree."

"Oh, no, you don't!" Using his hair blades, Vizor fires off a blue twister at Vanessa. She teleports out of the way. It's headed at the redwood now! D steps in and twirls his pendulum in his hands so swiftly that it fires the tornado back at Vizor, who promptly sidesteps.

"That was close..." Vizor whistles, pretending that never happened.

"Vanezzzzza..." Aria finally articulates in her psycho form.

"Just stay away. Just stay away!" She fires off more projectiles. Aria shreds them with her hair.

"Let uzzzzzz play..." Aria slashes at her once more.

"I have no time for games, and you know that." Vanessa creates a shockwave with her staff. The bleeding on her mouth has finally dried.

"ChcchChCHChzzz."

Aria notices Vanessa put everything she had into that shockwave and seizes the chance. She finally gets the fatal blow she's been looking for... Huh?

"It izzzzzz done."

Are you kidding? No, it isn't! Vanessa just fell over from blood loss, but you didn't even hit her.

"You only shredded her staff to bits!" I wind up my wings to give Vanessa the fatal blow I was picturing, but Aria stands in the way.

"And that is all I need to do to punish her. She can't control her powers without it." Aria's voice returns to normal, but her face, hair, and demeanor don't. "I cannot do any more for her. The rest is up to you."

"What are you talking about?"

Without a warning, Aria sends her hair through her back and out her stomach. The color of her eyes fades. Her hair stops spinning. She falls motionless to the ground.

"No! Not another!" Out of the darkness of space, the Unknown Phantom descends with her feminine voice. She grabs Aria's lifeless body. "Wake up. Get up, Aria, honey! … Please?" Aria's eyes haven't closed. You can still see the white of her eyes. "Why? How many comrades must you kill before we bring you back?"

"Comrades? You mistake me, grandmother."

Hold on. What? Grandmother. Wait. Vanessa is talking to…?

The Unknown Phantom removes her metal mask and fake hair, revealing a floating human spirit with a heavily wrinkled face. "You knew? It wasn't insanity blinding you when I told you a hundred times I was the Unknown Phantom? It wasn't enough for you to take the ghosts I was protecting and turn them into mud piles? You knew I was here the whole time? And you still refused to come into my arms? Me? Your own grandmother?"

Vanessa reaches for a sharp piece of her staff. "You should be… taking that reactor to Earth. That's all that matters… right now. Take it… and carry out my… plan."

No. No! No! No! NO! I won't let her kill herself too! I grab her right arm. "Stop. No more death."

"Just… let me… do what I must."

I finally realize what Aria meant. "No. You don't fear being killed. At all. You didn't even hesitate to grab that sharp edge. Why should I let you do anything you want to do? Your mind is so twisted that you probably can't even walk straight. Is that all life is to you? Just some game you can control with your power? And the SECOND it runs out, you bail because you know you lost? No way. Death is not the worst possible punishment for you. Because you won't learn anything by killing yourself, but you will learn by staying alive."

I knee her in the forehead, knocking her out.

– *Dark Spirit. Go and find Rod in that redwood. Bring him here.*

– *What? But your powers, they'll drain you.*

– Just do it.

– … Okay. As you wish.

The Dark Spirit leaves my body. I've got to find that tape, fast. Otherwise, this power is going to kill me. Come on, it's got to be on Vanessa somewhere… There! Her inside robe pocket. There's so much blood on it that I doubt it works anymore, but, just to be safe.

"Queen!" Rod acts worried. "Are you all right?"

"She's fine, Rod." I turn to him.

"What have you done to her?" He goes to punch me. I reveal the tape in my hands. "How did you get that?"

"Here, take it. Do what you want with it." I dismissively toss it to him.

Using both hands, he crushes it into nothingness. "Oh, V… thank you so much! It's so good to be back." He lunges out and hugs me.

"Be back? What do you mean?"

– Dark Spirit! Please, I'm about to pass out!

– I'm here. I'm here.

– Whew… thanks. A new form is always hard to adapt to right away.

– I imagine.

"We'll look for Nexus together! Back on Earth. Come on, let's go." This guy is loony.

"I actually have no idea what you're talking about."

"What? You're joking, right? Good one, V. Ahahahaha!"

"Buddy, I never knew you before I came to the Space Garden."

"What…?" Rod lets go of me. He backs up slowly and flies away.

"That was trippy."

"Hey, you. Dragon boy. V, was it?" Orient calls. I turn my head to face her. "I may not appreciate you knocking out my granddaughter with your fiery knee, but thank you kindly for teaching her a lesson."

"No worries. You did well, Orient."

"You know my name?"

"Of course. Aria told me."

"Aria…" Her watering eyes gaze at her corpse.

"Oh, sorry. I didn't mean–"

"No," she needs a moment to gather herself, "it's quite all right. I can face reality when I have to. This is one of those times." Wow, how wise. And how noble too. She stuck around all this time just to save her granddaughter. "Speaking of which, it's time I turned off that reactor, now that there's no kookoo granddaughter to tell me otherwise." Orient rises to the Phantom Reactor and flips the switch, shutting it down. With no power source to maintain itself, the reactor breaks down, piece by piece, and floats away into the recesses of space. "Good job, Neon. Aria. You both gave it your all. Now we're done. We'll have tea with each other now… for the rest of our afterlives." Orient blasts away. Aria's corpse, too, seems to have floated away. The only one that remains is Vanessa.

I look up to the sky. "I know what to do now, Aria. I'll help her." I throw Vanessa over my shoulder.

"V!" Azilez waves her hand from the redwood. I go to her, where Z, D, Griff, and Vizor are also waiting for me.

"The bodies inside the tree just fizzled. It seems the breaking of the reactor completely did them in." Vizor crosses his arms.

"But where's Aria?" Z asks.

I shake my head. "With Neon. And Orient." Everyone gasps. But that's it. Just a gasp. No tears. No fear. "She left Vanessa to us." I raise my shoulder, revealing the unconscious queen.

"What does that mean? SHE'S NOT DEAD?" Azilez rematerializes her rainbow hammer. I cut it in half with my wing. "V, STEP ASIDE. THIS HAS TO BE DONE! WHO KNOWS WHOM SHE'LL HURT NEXT?"

"I do." I reassure her that I have a plan.

"What does that mean?" Z is busy polishing his five iron, which is covered in different sponge cakes.

"It means we're letting her live."

"NO WAY. GIVE HER TO ME!" Azilez tries charging me to grab her. I press my wing on her forehead, preventing her from moving. Her arms and legs are still flailing.

"Look, I know it may sound crazy at first, but hear me out. Vanessa killed people once she got her powers from the Starlight Prophecies.

She just eliminated whatever problems she had, and she was even about to kill herself. She needs to realize that's not okay, and letting her die isn't the way to do it. Besides, if she does kill herself, she'll be free to terrorize others once again, without the limitations of a human body. Just look at the Unbound Evil. I wouldn't be surprised if Vanessa turned out like It if we don't turn her life around."

"You're too nice to her, V." Vizor flies up to me. "She doesn't deserve everything you're doing for her, but I guess I didn't either, so... I'm on board with this."

"Me too. That's a decent idea you got there, bud." Z rubs my hair, messing it up.

"It wasn't my idea. It was Aria's. Sort of like her last will."

"I. STILL. WANT. HER. HEAD!" Azilez is still flailing.

"Okay. You've done enough. You need a timeout." Griff grabs her arms.

"WHAT ARE YOU, MY MOM? LET ME GO!"

I'd say this is the perfect opportunity to head home.

Chapter 35

A Punishment Worse than Death

can barely describe what just happened these past few days, and, in some ways, I don't even want to. It was horrible, yet it wasn't at the same time. I'm trying to process it all in my head right now. And, still, we don't know anything about Nexus. Or was there something on the tape about him? One thing at a time, though. Let's give Vanessa her punishment.

"There. That should do it. Thanks, Jaclyn." I turn to the head scientist in charge of setting up Vanessa's "prison cell."

"What if she breaks out? Are you sure this is the best course of action? What if this little experiment of yours fails?" Jaclyn is concerned because I just told her about the experiences I had in the Space Garden. She really doesn't want Vanessa getting out of the strapped chair she's in.

"It won't. She's here, in an underground isolated room under Alcatraz, where all she can do is breathe and think. Even if she does break out, she has no powers anymore, and she can't get out without a security officer escorting her out. There's no way she'll break through ten feet of solid concrete without her former abilities." I try to make the last sentence sound as scientifically bulletproof as possible to calm her down.

"Yes! You are correct. Statistically speaking, it'll take a certain amount of…" Oh, boy, here she goes. Once you start talking science with Jaclyn, she'll never end the conversation. Let me explain what this "prison" is. As I just stated, it's in an underground, reinforced concrete room with nothing but a strapped chair. The chair is so tightly strapped that it's only really possible to move your head. I had the scientists and security place IVs inside Vanessa, to provide her with proper nutrition. All they have to do is replace the bags every week, and she'll never have to drink or eat again. "… And that's why it's impossible to break through this cement wall."

"Yeah, exactly." I nod, pretending I've been listening.

Jaclyn leaves through the security door to the surface. I tell her to give me a few minutes, so she swipes the door an extra time, allowing me to leave whenever I desire.

Vanessa finally wakes up, after being knocked out for two days. "… Where am I?"

"Back home. On Earth," I reply.

"Feels like it." She tries squirming around in her chair, but nothing happens. "Where's Orient?"

"Gone. Just like Neon and Aria. They all left."

"And Rod?"

"Who knows? He broke the tape you had and left."

"Figures."

"You're oddly composed for someone who's realizing she's going to spend the rest of her life in solitary confinement."

"Who cares? I've been doing that already. The only difference now is that I'm on Earth."

"I'm curious to see if you'll think that way in a week." I head for the door.

"Wait."

"What is it?"

"Can I see my parents?"

"Do you really want to?"

She looks at me with a blank stare. I can't tell if she's thinking or not. "… No."

"That's what I thought." I open the security door and look back at Vanessa one last time. Her hair is falling off, her skin is growing paler, and I can still see that scar across her mouth.

Chapter 36

White Sabbath

– VANESSA –

It's raining. I can hear the thunder cracking, lightning flashing. A building with a bell – what's it doing here? What does it mean? It's cold, made of stone. I go to touch it.

But what is this that stands in front of me? A figure in white. It's pointing at me. What do I do? Who is this? I panic. Out of fear, I run the other way, away from the building. That figure is chasing me. I can feel it. Even though I'm running, I can sense it's near. I can't see its eyes. Is it human? I don't know. I just don't know.

It's chanting something. "Chosen one... chosen one..." Me? The chosen one? No! No! No! I'm nobody. No one like me could ever be the chosen one.

AH! A fire's started! How? It's raining. There shouldn't be a fire in the rain! This makes no sense. Why is any of this happening, anyway? I'm more confused than afraid. There's nowhere to run.

Is this it? The end, my dear friends? Neon? Aria? Orient? ... Huh. I guess there's no one else to list. Not the most extensive list now, is it?

Hehehehehehe... HAHAHAHAHAHA!

Chapter 37
Doofus Links

Now that Vanessa is dealt with, it's time to sit back and relax. Well, until the government finds something else that looks fishy in the universe, anyway.

I look at my bedside clock: 8 am. "I think I'll sleep in today. It's raining right now, so I might as well wait until it blows over." Zzzzz… Zzzzz… Z…

"Z! GET BACK HERE!" So much for sleeping in. I trudge to my room's window and open the blinds. Azilez is chasing my older brother, who seems to have her brush in his hand.

"Tell me where my clubs are, and I'll give you your brush back."

"WHAT ARE YOU TALKING ABOUT? I DIDN'T TAKE THEM!"

"Well, I need them now, otherwise I can't practice for my tournament tomorrow." Z crosses his arms.

"Wait. You plan on practicing golf in this rain?"

"The course probably won't dry off in a day, so yeah. I'm going to practice in tournament conditions."

"I'm no golf expert, but even I know that's a recipe for a cold. NOW GIMME MY BRUSH!"

That's odd. I swear I saw Z's clubs in his room just yesterday. Let me check one more time, just to make sure.

Crreeeeeeaaaak. Z needs to fix the hinges on his door… and everything else. His room is easily the messiest in the tree house, other than Azilez's. I search his bedside, where I saw his clubs yesterday. Hmm… he's right. They're nowhere to be found. No robber could've taken them.

We would've sensed that. Who else would need golf clubs in this house? I walk downstairs through the living room and to the kitchen, where my mom is making eggs and pesto toast for Z.

"Hey, have you seen Z's clubs anywhere? Z says Azilez took them, and now they're having a hissy fit over it."

"D took them out about an hour ago. He said something about needing their rounded heads for something in his greenhouse."

"Ah. Thanks. I'll go get them and tell D to use something else."

I rush to D's greenhouse on the other side of the living room. This was a recent addition to the tree house. D always wanted his own garden, but he said that the constant San Francisco rain would mess with it. So we allowed him to get his own space for this. That's the best part about the tree house: adding a new room is as simple as waving Azilez's brush.

"D? Are you in here?"

"Yeah, I'm here. What do you need?" D is on the opposite end of this dirt-covered room. He's wearing oversized gray gloves and is totally barefoot. Sure enough, Z's clubs are right next to him, and he's got Z's four iron in his right hand.

"Z needs those clubs to practice today."

"In this rain?"

"THAT'S WHAT I SAID!" Uh oh. Azilez found us.

"Azilez, that's enough. It's not that big of a deal." Whoa, that was bizarre. Z is usually never so… authoritative. When it comes to golf, though, nothing can distract his focus.

"Okay…" Azilez twiddles her thumbs. Z hands her the brush. She darts to her room.

"Hey, D? Mind if I have those back?"

"Why do you need this set specifically? Can't you just create a set using your powers?" D is right. Z's done that plenty of times.

"Well, yeah, but this set is my set. It's the one that I perform best with. They're the clubs I'm most familiar with. I'm not going to play in a tournament using just any set of clubs."

"I never thought of it that way. If that's the case, can you whip up a four iron for me? It's great for tending this soil!"

"Sure." Z opens his right hand. Particles of light collapse in the form of a four iron. "Here." Z tosses the fresh four to D.

"Thanks! Here you go." D lifts the brown-and-green golf bag by its black handle and hands it to Z.

"Eww… what'd you do to them, D?" Z chuckles as he observes his four iron's head.

"Sorry! Here, let me clean them."

"Don't worry. There's rain outside. I'll wash them there."

D breathes a sigh of relief and waves goodbye with his pickaxe.

"Mom! Is my breakfast ready?" Z calls out.

"Yes, sweetie. Is Vizor coming?"

"One second, Mrs. Lara." Vizor hops down the stairs, trying to put on some of Z's golf pants. "Er… there!" Vizor's not going to play golf with Z, but he is going to be Z's caddie.

"Ready, Vi-ppphhorr?" Z asks as he stuffs a piece of toast in his mouth.

"I won't lie. I'm a little nervous. I feel as if I still don't understand the world of golf."

"Don't worry. No one ever fully understands it. Just remember the few pieces of advice I gave you: dress nice, stay quiet, and be support-ive. Golf is a grind, and any encouragement helps."

"I understand. I'll try my best."

I walk into the kitchen to grab some cereal.

"As least you're trying at all." Z raises his eyebrow, peering at me.

"Hey, there's no way I'm wearing those pants and collared shirt for five hours."

"Whatever you say, V." Z goes back to his toast.

Vizor grabs a bowl. Z, Vizor, and I eat our breakfast together. The rain lightens up after a while, so that's when Z and Vizor decide to head out.

Chapter 38

Fop 'n Floppin'
- VIZOR -

Why am I so jittery? It's only a game. No, wait, the tournament is tomorrow. This is only practice. What if I say something I shouldn't? What if I make a bad first impression? GAH! So many things that could go wrong!

"Hey, you okay, bud?" Z pats me on the back. "You're not coming down with another freezer already, are you?"

"No, no. I'm fine. It's just… I'm afraid of doing something I shouldn't. I don't want to make you, an expert, look bad."

"Don't worry about it. Everyone makes mistakes in golf, especially the players. You're helping me out so much just by being here. Trust me."

"Okay…" I still can't shake the feeling I'm about to royally screw things up.

"Up next on the tee… the 'Z' twosome," the speaker in the clubhouse blares.

"That's us. Let's go!" Z leaps from his chair, raring to go. I freezerishly follow.

The rain still isn't too bad as we walk onto the first tee. I carry Z's clubs on my back as I hand him his driver, ball, and wooden tee.

"All right, Vizor. What can you tell me about this hole?"

He's testing me already. That was fast. I shake my head, halting my internal monologue. I use my right hand to block the rain pelting my eyes. The hole goes straight initially, but then it veers to the left. "Umm... it's a dog-leg left. Watch out for the water hazard on the right side of the hole, so make sure to either hook the first shot or aim just right of that tree in the left rough."

"Excellent! I couldn't have said it better myself. See? You're doing fine. And that's all you have to do."

"Whew... I guess you're right!" I clench my fists in excitement.

"Excuuuuuse us, gentlemen." That was over-the-top. I don't think I've heard an accent that heavy, ever.

"Yes?" Z suddenly sounds professional. He puts his hands behind his back. That means I should as well.

"We are about to tee off as well, but couldn't help notice that you are also a twosome. Would you care to join us in our round today?" I know Z said we were supposed to dress fancy, but this seems too much. This man is wearing a top hat, a tight-fit, brown-buttoned jacket, and a monocle. He also has a giant French moustache.

"Sure." Z reverts to his casual self.

"Oh, riveting idea, darling." The woman next to him flicks her wrist downward. She is also wearing a monocle. However, her jacket is sportier than her husband's. That doesn't mean her attitude seems any less foppish.

"Allow us to introduce ourselves. I am Wellington. Charmed." He tips his hat.

"And I am Harriet. Delighted to meet you."

"I'm Z."

"Uhh... I'M VIZOR!"

"Oh, dear, my eardrums betray me!" Wellington holds his ears. "Can you kindly reduce your volume levels down a notch or two? I would highly appreciate it. This is a golf course after all, not a babysitting clinic."

"Ooooh..." What's this guy's deal? I'm nervous, and I raised my voice a little. So what? That doesn't give him the right to be high and mighty.

"Hey, if we don't hit our balls soon, the course warden will get mad." Z finishes his stretches.

"Oh, dear, you are correct. Well, then, let us begin, shall we?" Wellington and Harriet adjust their monocles as they place their legless bags on the ground.

"Vizor, what was that?" Z makes sure they can't hear us.

"They were just so imposing. It's like they think they're better than us."

"Don't worry. We'll shut them up." Z grasps his driver in both of his hands.

"How?"

"Oh, you'll see. I've played with characters like these before."

Z walks onto the tee furthest from the hole: the black-colored tees. He places his left index finger in between his right pinkie and ring finger, making sure to grip his club tight. He swings back, down, and a magnificent PING fills the air as he strikes his ball and follows through. The ball goes dead straight, over the tree in the rough, and lands on the fairway.

"Well, I say! Nice shot."

"Thank you, Wellington." Z hands me his driver, which I scrub off with a white towel that is attached to his bag. "You're up."

"Indeed." Wellington holds his wooden driver.

"Watch this, Vizor," Z whispers to me. I pay attention to Wellington's form. It's much different from Z's. It's more relaxed, in a way, almost lazy. He winds back and a broad THWAT rings in my ears.

"Oh, that sucked," I whisper back to Z.

"I know. That's what I meant earlier. People like this talk big, but never play to back it up. It's important to stay humble because you're not going to play amazing golf every day. It's just not possible for anyone, even pros."

"Excuse me? You talk 'humbly?'" I put in air quotes.

"Aha. You caught me. You know what I mean." We exchange laughs and move on. The rain gets heavier, and becomes a downpour by hole five. Wellington and Harriet stop playing. Honestly, we should've stopped playing too, but Z is determined to get through the round.

"This is when golf kinda bites you in the butt!" Z shouts over the rain. "The weather can completely change the tide of a match. Observe." Z hits his driver as hard as he can. It goes only 100 yards. By comparison, his normal driving distance is about 350 yards.

"So what now?"

"What we always do!" Z changes into his extreme form. The rain around him evaporates before it has a chance to hit the ground, due to the fire on his clubs when he grasps them. His eyes turn green, and his hair flies around. Kind of like how Wellington's moustache was reacting to the violent winds.

"Ah, yes! I've been waiting for this moment all day." I burst into my extreme form. My hair catches fire, my eyes become crimson, and my dark aura radiates.

"Let's keep going." Z continues to whack at his ball, despite the tornado-force winds. PING! PONG! GONG! The ball makes a different sound, depending on the club he uses, but they all sound like they should be put into a symphony. A symphony for victory! By the end of the round, not a single one of his shots had landed out of bounds. There were a few scares, but he recovered from all of them with grace. One of his shots even ended up in a lake, but it was shallow enough to walk in and hit it out.

"Ok, let's head home. Everyone's probably worried sick about us."

"Good idea," I concur. "Hopefully the weather won't be as bad for the tournament tomorrow."

Chapter 39

Tournament Time

I'm not sure how Vizor and Z got any practice done yesterday, considering our tree house almost blew away from the winds, but they seem energized and ready for today.

Z got up at 6 o'clock because his tee time is at 8. He wanted to make sure he has ample time to eat, get to the course, warm up, and rest between all of that and his tee time. The racket woke me up, so I decided to sleep for a little longer before my alarm goes off at 7:30.

– *Zzzzzz… Zzzzz… Zzzzz… hmm…*

– *What troubles you, V?* The Dark Spirit asks.

– *The alarm should've rung by now. Let's see… huh? Where is it?*

– *It wasn't Me. That's certain.* The Dark Spirit was inside me the whole night, so that's an ironclad alibi.

– *Well, it doesn't matter who took it. We could be late!* I jump out of my sheets and check my phone, sitting on top of my TV. Oh, jeez! It's 7:50! I'm gonna miss his tee time.

"Go! Go! Go!" I rinse my mouth, brush my teeth, and put my black-and-red shoes on. Now it's 7:55. Whew! I'll get there in time.

I run out of my door, only to bump into Griff, who is waiting for me. He tumbles on the floor.

"Sorry, buddy. You okay?"

"Ah. Yeah. Don't worry. But come on! Hop in my car, or we're gonna miss Z tee off."

"Your car? Your toy collection doesn't count."

"No, no, Azilez made one for me. It'll hover in the air and fly at sonic speed. Everyone else left already."

"Then there's no more time to lose. Lead the way!" We rush down the stairs and open the entrance, where Griff's car is already hovering. Nice convertible! It has an orange hood with a white stripe in the middle that extends out once it reaches the headlights. The rest of the frame is orange, but the doors are white.

We hop in, and he floors it.

"It's 7:58. Awesome! We'll make it." I check my phone once more.

Griff lowers his car into a parking spot and we rush inside the clubhouse, where the receptionist is assisting other frantic latecomers.

"Excuse us, but where do spectators go to watch the tournament?"

"Out this door to your right, and follow the blue signs."

"Awesome. Thank you." Griff slams ten dollars onto the desk to pay for the spectator fee, grabs two badges, throws one at me, and charges out the open door. "There he is."

"Up next on the tee, from beautiful San Francisco, California… Z!"

"GO, Z!" Azilez jumps up and down. Our families are standing behind her.

"Shhhhh!" Other spectating parents glare at her.

"Eh… you want your three wood, right? You said the tailwind might carry your ball into the rough?" Vizor wants to clarify.

"Yup. Good job, bud. You're getting the hang of this." Z gives a noogie just above Vizor's forehead.

Vizor hands Z his three wood, and Z tees up his ball. He takes a deep breath as he adjusts his grip. He takes his club back and… THWAT! Eww… that didn't sound good. That's going way left. It goes left of the tree in the rough and gets caught in a bush.

"Ugh… Okay, okay. Not the best start. No big deal." Z hands his club back to Vizor. Griff and I rush over to Azilez's side.

"Hey, guys! You just missed Z goof up his first shot of the tournament."

"Actually, we were standing right over yonder. We just didn't want to make any noise, unlike some OTHER people."

"What is that supposed to mean?"

"Shhhhhhh!" The same parents glare at her again.

"That. That's what it's supposed to mean."

"Fine, you've made your point." Azilez hangs her head down. We follow Z to his ball, making sure not to talk to him because of tournament rules.

"Boy, it's really… *THWIP*… dug in there." Vizor hacks at the bush with his hair blades, trying to make the ball hittable so Z doesn't have to take a stroke penalty. "Aha! Got it."

"Good work, caddy." Z claps. "Now hand me my seven iron."

Vizor twists his upper body toward the bag and reaches for the recently shined seven iron. Z grabs it with more confidence than that shot warrants.

Z takes a look at the bush. It's covering where a right-handed hitter would normally stand. Vizor can't cut the whole bush, only a part of it. After all, it's a part of the course. "I knew something like this would happen someday. So I came prepared. Vizor, hand me my eight iron."

"There are two of them in here… Oh! I get it. One of them is lefty."

"Bingo. And that's exactly how I'm going to hit."

"That's risky, though. You haven't really practiced that, have you?"

"I mean, even if I use a right-handed club, it's not going to go very far anyway."

"That's a good point. All right, let's try it." Vizor hands Z the lefty eight iron. He makes sure to grip the club tight so he can fight some of the shrub still surrounding the ball. THWAT! That didn't sound good either. Oh, wait. The ball is running across the ground. It might not have gone in the air, but it's headed toward the hole!

"Go. Go. Go!" my dad murmurs to himself. "Yeah! All right. He can go up and down from there." The ball stops about 20 yards from the hole. Vizor and Z exchange high-fives.

"What hole are we on? I wanna go home." Azilez is growing impatient.

"It's only hole seven. There are 11 more after this." I walk beside her. She groans.

"The headwind is kicking up a bit." Z plucks some grass off the tee box and drops it. The wind pushes it back into D, who revels in it. "I'll need my driver this time." Vizor follows Z's command. Ball's set, wind up, and... PING!

"Finally! First good tee shot today." Z picks up his tee. "See, Vizor? That's what I meant when I said golf could be tough at times. You may not hit well all the time, but a great golfer can bounce back at any time."

"Intriguing... It's like a war."

"How so?" Z throws his driver back into the bag.

"Well, the tide can turn at any moment. One crucial move, or in this case shot, can rejuvenate the fighting spirit. On the flip side, one slip-up can spell the end of your life."

"The consequences in golf aren't that severe, but they can sure feel like that sometimes."

"Well, then, you'll have to tell me about those sometime." The two exchange smiles and continue walking on the fairway.

Believe it or not, Z is actually the last one coming off the course for the tournament. Yeah, an 8-o'clock tee time is LATE, apparently. There was no way Azilez's attention span would make it through 18 holes, so she created a floating rainbow board and fell asleep on it. And I'm the one pulling it.

But the pressure's on now. It's the end of the 18th hole, and if Z can get the ball into the hole in two shots, he'll win the tournament. If he hits three, though, he'll tie with the current leader, Harriet, and they'll have to play sudden death. From the looks of it, that is something Z does not want to do 'cause he is sweating bullets.

That's the cool part about this sport, though. You can't tell if his sweat is from being tired or feeling pressured.

"Vizor, lob wedge."

"Here you are."

"Go time." Z walks up to his ball on the back fringe. He opens his clubface, signaling that he's going for a flop shot. That makes sense. The green is going downhill, so he wouldn't want the ball to roll as much. The wind up looks good, but oh, no. It's long! "Bite! Bite!" Z grates his teeth. As if heeding his call for help, the headwind kicks up at the ball's maximum height and blows it back just enough to where it's short of the hole by five feet. Z lets out a fist pump.

"All right. This is the moment of truth. Hand me my put–"

The wind suddenly grows furious, sort of like it was yesterday.

"WHOA!" Okay, forget what I said. This wind is nothing like yesterday's. I can barely hear myself over this. What's going on?

A yellow laser blasts from the sky and strikes San Francisco. Even though we took every precaution, I can't help but think this has something to do with Vanessa. Z grasps his putter like a sword now, and Vizor has his hair blades in his hands.

"Azilez. Azilez. Azilez!" I continuously pat her cheek until she wakes up.

"Huh? What? Is it over? Did he win?" She rubs her eyes. Or at least she tries until the wind knocks her off her board. "Owie! What's with the wind lately?"

"I think we have bigger problems, guys." Griff points to the distance, where a myriad of airships that look exactly like Vizor's hair blades fill the sky. San Francisco is being attacked!

Chapter 40

The Project's Purpose

"**Q**uick! Let's head downtown." I lead the chaos-powered pack. "Most of the ships seem to be there. Vizor, what's going on?"

"I'm as confused as you, V. I thought the rest of my people went extinct when the Devil absorbed them all on our last adventure. Those are Treah's ships for sure, though."

Brrrriinnnngg… brrrriiinnnnnnnnggg… really? At a time like this? Who could be…? Oh. It's Jaclyn.

"Yes?"

"V. Come to the military post on Yerba Buena Island. It appears the past presidents were keeping a secret from Project Mutant."

"What? Okay, I'll be right there."

"Don't fret, V. We'll take care of everything here," Vizor reassures.

"Thanks." I veer off to the coast of Yerba Buena Island, located in the heart of San Francisco Bay.

"Ah, good. You are here. Come, we must make haste." Jaclyn grabs my arm and runs inside. She punches a code into an elevator. It opens immediately. After going a few stories underground, it opens to a room with a single wooden table. On that table, there's an old laptop. There is only one light bulb dangling from the ceiling. Two soldiers stand firm on each side of the elevator.

"Welcome, Mr. V," the soldier on the left salutes me. I do my best to salute back.

"Ever since the arrest of the latest president, we've been searching the Oval Office for any hidden substances, and, sure enough…" She clicks on the spacebar. "We find this file, which has Project Mutant's code number on the top right of the page."

I examine the screen. The rug has been removed from the White House floor, and right in the middle of the room, there is a one-foot-by-one-foot-square incision, revealing a sheet of paper. It looks like a preschooler drew on it, though. "There's just a bunch of black lines on the page."

"It may not look important to the naked eye, but run it under an ultraviolet light scanner, and you get this!" She presses on the spacebar once more. Now the page looks like a bird's-eye-view map of a building. The front of the building looks familiar.

"It's a map of the White House. But that's it. It's just a map. There's nothing special about it, right?"

"That's what we initially concluded as well, but then I asked what a map of the White House was doing inside Project Mutant's folder. And, more importantly, why was it under the Oval Office? Someone was hiding this." She has a point there. And that's a pretty good hiding spot. No one would suspect anything there. "So, in addition to the ultraviolet scanner, we ran the map under an infrared scanner and found this." Now things are getting interesting. The entire paper is blue, except for one red spot above the room that is labeled "cold storage."

"Did you find anything in there related to Project Mutant?"

"Not inside the room, no. But UNDER the room, yes." She clicks the spacebar a third time. She reveals a cassette tape under the center of the room.

"What were its contents?" Great, now she has me talking all science-y too.

"It was tough to crack. Playing it on a normal TV would just cause an ear-bleeding high pitch. It would likely deafen whoever listened to it. A clever safety measure for something you need to hear to figure out. We needed to run it through a frequency-lowering device. And, finally, this is the missing content of Project Mutant."

Jaclyn plays the ominous audio message.

"This *bzzzzzrrtt* is your final warning *bzzzzrrrtt*. My patience is growing thin. *bzzzzzzzzrrrrttt* If you don't find those five glowing *bzzzzzzrrrtt* yellow rocks in the next ten years, then *bzzzzzrrtt* your planet will cease to exist."

That was an Omoh sapien!

"I have been employed by the US government far before Project Mutant. Even to me, the concept was… unnecessary. There was no reason to turn our own into monsters."

"So not even security was trusted with this secret? They were just told what to do about it?"

"It would seem so. I speculate this threat is the fleet that is attacking us now."

"Thank you for the information, Jaclyn." I bow. "I'll be on my way now. My friends need my help."

"Go forth, then." She puts her hands behind her back. "I'll try to find out more here, if I can."

Chapter 41

Flooding the Fleet

All the action is still localized to the downtown area. That's good. It must mean that my friends and family are putting up a valiant resistance. Time to join them!

I zoom across the water, creating skyscraper-sized splashes behind me. The golden-blade ships are still firing at the downtown area, destroying everything in sight. I'd react more melancholy to this, but Azilez's brush can just fix everything later. As long as everyone in the city was evacuated in time...

– *Like you have to ask.* Vizor flies next to me from the horizon. He must've taken everyone to safety using his purple sphere, like he did last time the city was attacked.

"Nice job. Now let's send these Omoh sapiens packing!"

"Let's." Vizor takes his blades out from his hair and goes ahead of me.

"Shields, up!" Azilez spawns more rainbow shields of varying sizes to protect as much of the city as she can.

"Come down here and fight us!" Griff's hair burns the incoming lasers to smithereens. He shakes his fist at the fleet.

"V, glad you finally made it. Here, take this twig, and–." Before D can finish giving me instructions, the airships retreat. "Huh?" D squints to see if he can spot any more ships, but can't.

"That was strange."

"They must've known I was coming." Vizor grins.

"Right..." Azilez blasts him with yellow paint. "Did you know

THAT was coming?"

"Why you…! Get over here." Vizor chases her around the ruined city, as if the ships had never come.

"Guys, knock it off. We have to go after that fleet!" I have a feeling this is far from over.

"Why?" Z asks. "They left willingly. Besides, I need to go back and make my tournament-winning putt."

I let everyone know what I heard from Jaclyn. The important stuff, anyway. I leave out the parts about the ultraviolet and infrared rays. There's just no time. We could all be in serious danger. I ask Vizor to go check on Vanessa.

"It just dawned on me, but those ships were after the Starlight Prophecies, right?"

"It actually could've been the Vanity Prophecies," Z points out.

"No. It couldn't have. This message is ten years old. The Vanity Prophecies are younger than that. Vanessa made them from her brother. Do we know who currently has the Starlight Prophecies?"

"GUUUUUUUYS!" Vizor's voice booms. "Vanessa's gone!"

"As I feared." I cross my arms. "That whole laser light show was a distraction. We were played for fools."

"Well, how about we stop dawdling and go get her back?" Vizor grows antsy.

"Good call. Let's go!"

"Do you see them?" We zip across the solar system.

"There! In the Kuiper Belt," Vizor points.

"Let's nail 'em!" Azilez spawns her board and descends to the ships. We fly at her side.

"How do we know which ship she's in?" D asks as we get closer.

"We'll just have to invade them all." I land on the bottom deck on the ship in the back. An army of Omoh sapiens meets us there.

"Halt! Who goes there?" The Omoh sapien at the helm steps up.

"Me, you dolts," Vizor speaks. They all gasp.

"What are you doing off of Treah?" One of the soldiers shakes.

"Orders by my father. I've been sent here to stop you."

– *But your dad's dead.*

– *They don't know that. I remember who these guys are: a fleet of rebels. They tried overthrowing my father when he became king. Something about not agreeing with his political ideologies. Anyway, my father pounded their resistance to the ground and banished them to space.*

– *Way to go off the fly, buddy.* I compliment him.

"But all of the Omoh sapiens from Treah– mmm!"

I cover Azilez's mouth. "Shh! Just play along for now, okay? Blink once so I know you understand." She blinks twice. "Eh, you tried."

"What? It's dry in space!"

"Now are you all going to give up? Or am I going to have to teach you your place for my father?"

"How adorable." The ship from up front slows down and makes the cockpit visible. A scrawny figure with silver hair blades, white cape, and wooden teeth is piloting it.

"And who are you?"

"Plaplaplaplapla! You don't remember? 'Cause I remember you, Vizor! Son of Syzor the Second."

"Give me a break. You were banished when I was like 100. I was merely told your story. Do you have any idea how old I am now?"

"I should be asking *you* that question. Plapla!" That is the most artificial laugh I have ever heard. "They call me Scrougholwer, boy-o. And I'm about to crank this baby into maximum overdrive."

SHHHHRRRREEEEEE!

Where'd they all go? And, more importantly, where did Z, D, Vizor, Azilez, and Griff go?

Chapter 42

Adifoahqwekrqoeifhehadilsdk Isjeklsidhpaoep

'm back home? But I was just at the Kuiper Belt. I can't move that fast.

Oh, no. She must've gotten control again. "I'm in all sorts of trouble now" is what I would say if I didn't have the Dark... huh?

– *Dark Spirit? Are You there?* No reply. – *Come on. This isn't funny. Vanessa's at it again. Say something!* It's all in vain. I can't sense It anywhere. In fact, I can't sense anything. If I try, I feel burned by an astronomically intense light.

At least I still have my ultimate form, though. I typically don't go all out from the get-go, but with Vanessa, anything is possible. So I don't want to be caught off guard again. Hrrrrrraaa– uhh... what? I CAN'T TRANSFORM EITHER? How is that possible? Even if the prophecies are locked away from me, their powers are still within... OW! Oh, I see. I can't look inside myself at all. That's low, Vanessa. The "if I can't do it, no one can" strategy. At this point, though, what else can I expect from her?

"All right, I'll play along in your little game. Happy?" I'm in a damp place. I think it's a wetland. There's a two-story box-shaped house in front of me. I wonder if this place means anything to Vanessa.

With nothing else to do, I walk inside. "Hello?" I holler. "Hello?" Nothing. Silence. It's so quiet that you can hear the dust bouncing off the wooden walls.

This living room looks comfy. There's a big, brown couch with an old-fashioned CRT TV and a cassette player. I spy a remote nestled in between the couch cushions. I pick it up and reluctantly turn the TV on.

BZZZZZZZZZ… "Go upstairs," the black TV screen says in Vanessa's torn voice. Bleeeeeeeeppp… The remote in my hand vanishes.

"What is this? If you're trying to scare me, it won't work." A bowl of fruit falls off the coffee table in front of the couch. "AHH! Oh."

I try walking outside again, but when I open the door, the light outside burns. I immediately close it so I don't go blind. My breathing grows heavier. Calm down… don't let her rattle you, V. None of this is real. It's all an illusion.

"Go upstairs…" Vanessa's torn voice is getting sharper.

"Why should I?" The walls grow spikes and close in on each other. "OKAY! OKAY! Geez. Ever so pushy you are." I run upstairs. There are three rooms up here. Hmm… I feel like if I go into the wrong one, I'll die. Or she can just rig them all. I'm gonna go with that.

I open the first door to my left. There's a king-sized bed in there with three layers of sheets on it. One blue, the other red, and the top one is white. The wall behind it is completely blank, but to the left of the bed there's a window. I look outside and see total darkness. There's one other thing in the room, a bronze metallic dresser with six drawers. Nothing is on top of it, so I begin opening the drawers one by one. The first five have nothing in them, but the final one has a ruby pendant with a rusted picture frame beside it. I pick up both objects and observe the photo inside the frame closer. That's Aria! And are those supposed to be her mom and dad? I can't tell. Their bodies are there, but where are their heads?

CLICK! It sounds like another room is unlocked.

I go to the middle of the three rooms now. This looks like a kid's playroom. There is a single beanbag in the center, with two mugs beside it. Inside those mugs, there's hot chocolate. Some of it is hardened around the rims. They've been sitting there for a while. Scattered across the room are large, multicolored alphabet blocks. I look back at the room's entrance. The door is closed. That's strange, I don't remember closing it. Four red alphabet blocks sit at the base, spelling "ARIA."

CLICK. The last room is unlocked. Do I even dare?

I press on. The final room is another bedroom, but this one is smaller. If I were to guess, the first room belongs to Aria's parents and this one belongs to Aria herself. Speaking of Aria, she's staring into the black window at the very back of her room. She still has her metal hair.

I call out to her.

She turns around. Her eyes are completely white. Her face, expressionless. "Yes?" I can sense her spirit! But how? She flew away after... you know.

"Why are you here? I thought you were done with Vanessa."

"Vanessa?" She tilts her head. "Who is that?"

"Your best friend?" I don't like where this is going.

"Oh, you must mean Neona." NO! How can Vanessa do this to her?

I try storming out of the room, but after opening the door, I'm greeted with another blinding light, which forces me to close it.

"Aria, snap out of it. Vanessa is blinding you with her power. Don't let her!"

"Again with this 'Vanessa.' I already told you, her name is Neona." Her voice grows sterner. It seems like Vanessa is controlling more than just her memory. Maybe I can get her mad to the point where she messes up her illusion.

"Nope. Definitely Vanessa."

"NO. NEONA."

"Vanessa."

"NEONA."

"Vanessa."

"NEONA!"

"Vanessa."

"NEONA! FOR THE LAST TIME, IT'S NEONA!" Aria goes psycho and her hair destroys her house. Her eyes are still blank, though. We now find ourselves in a white field. Everything is white. The ground, the sky, the walls... all of it. "NO ONE WILL BE ALLOWED TO REMEMBER. THERE IS ONLY NEONA."

"So you are controlling her, then."

"Sure, whatever. I'm controlling her." Aria's voice becomes Vanessa's.

"What does it prove? You're going to play with me forever anyway. With no powers at your disposal, you won't run away this time."

"Who said I was running from you? I was chasing you. I'm not afraid of you, nor are my friends."

"Oh, I wouldn't say that."

"What have you done to them?"

"Me? Nothing I won't regret."

"THAT'S IT. YOU CAN LASH AT ME ALL YOU WANT AND TAKE ALL MY POWERS AWAY, BUT USING MY CLOSEST FRIENDS AS INSUR-ANCE IS PATHETIC." Even though Vanessa's illusion has put a barrier between my conscious self and my soul, my evil form seeps through and surfaces. Evil V is back, but this time, I'm in control. The white eyes, the single red blot in the center of each, the white steam from my eyes, and the crimson aura and grin.

"What's this? How is this happening? This isn't a part of the illu-sion! How are you doing that?"

"EVIL IS NO ILLUSION. IT'S REAL. JUST LIKE THIS BEATING YOU'RE ABOUT TO GET!"

"Is that so? Let us see you try!" Vanessa's voice becomes Aria's psycho voice again. She slashes at me with her hair. I don't move out of the way. She needs to see she can't hurt me. When Aria draws near, I grab her titanium hurricane hair with my bare hands. Her hair stops, and my hands don't have a scratch.

I flip her onto the ground with enough force to shatter the white floor beneath her. I then flip her onto my opposite side. And again, and again, and again, and again, until her breath becomes so shaky that I can mistake it for an old car engine. "VANESSA, YOU WILL LEAVE HER BODY THIS INSTANT."

"You're so mean, you know that?"

I stay silent out of curiosity about what she'll say next.

"You pound me into the ground, thinking I'm Neona. But I'm Aria. What have I done to deserve this? You're lashing out on someone who helped you through your journey at the Space Garden."

"OH, NO… YOU'RE RIGHT. LOOKS LIKE I SCREWED UP.

HERE, LET ME RUB SOME SALT ON THOSE WOUNDS." I throw her up into the air, and, as she descends, I axe-kick her into the already-cracked floor, destroying it completely. BOOOOOOOOOOM! I literally just tore through the illusion. The white everything implodes on itself, and after another flash of light, I find myself back in Aria's room, perfectly intact. Aria is lying on the floor, face down. I reach for her, but her body melts, revealing that it was made from Syrusima. Her spirit is revealed, but it has no soul. She plops forward onto the carpet floor. I cradle her spirit, hoping it's not too late to reverse the brainwashing effects. "Aria, say something!" My evil form abruptly subsides. I can't feel it anymore.

"V..." She remembers me! That's a good sign.

"Thank goodness you're okay. Do you know where we are?"

"Where... we are?" Her voice softens. "I used to know. But now... it's all a nightmare. A nightmare... I can't forget... because it's all... I know." She falls out of my arms, back onto the floor. I shed tears.

"How? How can people do this to someone? Are they never satisfied? How can they do this to those who comfort? To those who nurture? To those who protect? To those who fight? To those who follow their friends to the ends of the galaxy just to see if they're okay? Now Aria's in eternal torment. Her spirit will always live on, and she'll always feel dead inside. Worst of all, there's nothing I can do about it. And I'm right next to her."

Another bright light flashes. I'm taken to a different location.

Chapter 43

8q3ijofjspjoer03`832ro`93hrend 99ejeie9danlviz

Now what? Now whom are you going to torture just because you can, Vanessa? You might as well just tell me and get it over with. I can't watch this anymore. It sickens me to no end, thinking you can toy with your friends even after they're already dead. Just let them be. I gave you a second chance so you can see just how much of your own life you're throwing away, so you can start over, but it seems you're obsessing. Nothing will sate you. You'll always want more.

Whoa, I didn't expect THIS. A massive mansion with a 20-foot-tall silver door surrounded by an iron fence. Hold on, this looks familiar. This is Vanessa's house on Earth, isn't it? Maybe she heard my internal monologue and is finally ready to put her old ways aside and face me one-on-one.

And that's when I realize she has a brother. And a grandmother.

But I have to press forward. My friends could be in danger!

I walk up to the iron fence. As I am thinking of how to get it open, it automatically opens, tempting me to enter. In between the fence and the front door, there is actually some lovely shrubbery and well-maintained grass fields surrounding the mansion. It's almost enough to make me forget the eternal purgatory Vanessa is creating for her friends. Almost.

The silver door opens, and, inside, I see three mahogany, velvet-lined staircases, each leading to a different corridor. On this ground floor, there is only a path that leads to a restaurant-sized kitchen. Behind that, there is a glass door leading outside, which, like before, leads to darkness. The door closes behind me. I'll just go upstairs right away. There's no point dawdling down here.

That's when I look up and see that the stairs are gone. And without the ability to feel my soul, I can't go up. Looks like Vanessa is forcing me to take the long, twisted road. She's trying to break me.

"You're acting lame, you know. I'm just gonna look around, find some stuff, and you're going to just put the stairs back to where they were." No reply from her at all. "I know you're there, so listen up. I gave you a second chance at life, and this is what you did with it? I hope you're happy, because when I get my hands on you, you'll finally realize the weight of your sins. And they'll crush you! Do you hear me?" I lose my cool a little on that last bit, but recompose and move forward to the kitchen. There are five different ovens, each with their own stovetops. Five crockpots sit on those stovetops, waiting to be opened. This time, I'm wrong. There's nothing in any of them. "Okay, so now you're gonna be cryptic about this too? How lovely. I can't wait to end you."

I notice there's a side hallway at the left end of the kitchen, so I try that next. One of the doors is already open. I walk inside, hoping to find something so I can get a move on. It's a laundry room. There's simple tile flooring, with a washer and a dryer sitting side by side. Inside the dryer, I find a fluffy, newly-knit, blue sweater. THUMP! I think those were one of the flights of stairs. Finally!

I walk to the entrance. The left staircase has been put back. I trudge upward. There are… TEN ROOMS? Okay, fine. Let's see what's in these. Crreeeeaaak. Well, this one leads to a wall. Crreeeeeaaaak. This one too. All of them lead to walls? Well, maybe not this last one, considering it's at the end of the hall. Whew, good. There's actually something in this one. Imagine if this was all just a trap and I actually needed to go and find something else downstairs. Things should be smooth sailing from here. Emphasis on "should be." I don't get my hopes up – as a defensive measure, just in case.

The last door leads to what looks like a maid's sleeping chambers. There's an old cot on the far-right end of this narrow, peeling, wooden room, and a frilly, black maiden outfit is hung on the entrance. This furnace on the left is a little jarring, though, considering it's in a wooden room. Does this part of the mansion just not get any heat from the ventilation? No way can it be from lack of money. Their front door is made of silver. But I have a feeling I know where I can find the next key item.

I open the furnace. Sure enough, it's been used recently, and there's a picture of Orient in here. Vanessa's parents made their own parents work as maids for them? I guess the apple doesn't fall too far from the tree.

THUMP! There goes another set of stairs. Time for the middle staircase.

This hall looks much like the last one: nine doors on the sides, with one more at the end. I'm not even going to bother with the side doors. Let's just go straight to the... are you kidding me? The door at the end of the hall is a dead end this time? Fine, I'll open the other doors.

Nine, eight, seven, six, five, four, three, two, and one.

This time, the door closest to the stairs is the correct door. This one leads to a butcher. I guess it's handy to have it close to the kitchen, so the maids don't have to constantly walk long distances. There are bricks on all four walls and even the floor. The carving table is made of granite. Understandable, since you wouldn't want to cut on top of something more valuable. The scent of fresh blood fills the air, as something seems to be on top of the table. I say "seems" because I can't actually see the top of the table. It's completely blacked out. Maybe there's a light switch for it? Where would it be? I don't see anything on the walls. Maybe on the... ceiling. Ughhhhh. It bothers me that I can't just jump up and tap it. Or can I? I lean against the entrance, get a running start, and, OOF! The darkness blocks me. It seems I'll need a long tool of some sort to flick it open. I remember seeing a long, wooden pizza peel in the kitchen. I'll use that.

Okay, I have it in my hands, and I'm back upstairs. Time to turn on the light. It's just cubes of mea... AHHHHHHHHHHHH! IT SPELLS "VENISS!" IS THAT ACTUALLY NEON'S... UGH... MY STOMACH. I

DON'T WANT TO IMAGINE IT. I'm not even going to say it.

THUMP! The last staircase.

Again, like the last two corridors, this one is structured the same. Since the second corridor's correct door was the first door in the hall and the first corridor's correct door was the final door, I think this corridor's will be the fifth door down. AHA! … Oh. I guess I'm not that clever. Okay, I'll just close this door and try the–

RGHRGHRGHRGHRGH.

All the doors just shook. That's not good. What can it mean? Let me try another door and see if it happens–

RGHRGHRGHRGHRGH.

So now it's just random. And if I get it wrong, the rooms reshuffle? Great. So it's a guessing game. Excuse me while I play "Eenie meanie miney mo" with myself.

Is it this one? No.

RGHRGHRGHRGHRGH.

C'mon… it's this one! No.

RGHRGHRGHRGHRGH.

Maybe this one?

RGHRGHRGHRGHRGH.

It's gotta be this one.

RGHRGHRGHRGHRGH.

Please… this one? Ugh.

RGHRGHRGHRGHRGH.

It's been… so long. Come on. This one… it must be. Yes! About time.

I don't even care what room this is anymore; just get me out of here. Where's the final item? Oh, wait. The final room's key items aren't items. They're people. Well, a person. Orient's here. And just like Aria, her eyes and face are lifeless.

"What are you doing here, little V? Get out! I've got to tend to Neona," she snaps for no reason.

"Are we really going to have the same conversation we had back at Aria's house?"

"What are you jabbering on about? I never went there. There's no time to ever go there, what with working as a maid 'n all."

"Okay, look. We know exactly how this is going to go down. You're going to say that your name is Neona, I'm going to say it's Vanessa, you're gonna get heated, and I'm going to whip your butt to kingdom come. So why don't we just skip to that last phase and speed up this process? I spent too much time just getting in here."

"Did you eat kookoo nuts for breakfast this morning? I've never heard anyone spout that kind of nonsense since I was a lass. And that was almost a century ago!" Orient shakes her fist at me.

I take a deep breath. There's no way around it. This is going to be a repeat performance of last time. "The only breakfast I ate was the one coming from Vanessa's kitchen."

"Vanessa? You mean Neona."

"Vanessa."

"Neona."

"Vanessa."

"NEONA."

"Vanessa."

"NEONA!"

"Vanessa… *yaaaaawwwn*"

"FOR THE LAST TIME, IT'S NEONA." Orient transforms into the Unknown Phantom. The energy surge destroys the mansion. Also as with Aria, the white field is back. "How are you going to fight me without ANY powers? There's no way anything will break through now. So we're playing on my terms, okay? Okay. Great! Teehee." The Unknown Phantom's voice becomes Vanessa's.

"You're forgetting something, though." I got to do some thinking during my hour-long journey of opening doors.

"Oh? What's that?" Vanessa asks.

"See, your illusions aren't yours. They're the Starlight Prophecies'. And guess who can wield the power of the Starlight Prophecies too?"

"GRrRRrRrrRRr!" The Unknown Phantom rusts away. Her insane

self is finally revealed: a corrupted computer glitch with Vanessa's dis-jointed limbs and head with pitch-yellow eyes. "YoU caNNOt conTROL theM. nO onE CaN." Her voice adapts with her transformation. It sounds like a computer had been shredded but is still making glitching noises.

She rushes me at sonic speed.

"You're too slow!" My extreme form surfaces from the power of the Starlight Prophecies.

"NoOooOOOOo!"

"Call off your little mirage and I'll call off my extreme form."

The white field implodes on itself again, and now I'm floating in space. I can see Earth in front of me.

"Don't think for a second that this is over!" a mighty voice echoes from behind. I turn around.

– *What IS that?* I can feel the Dark Spirit flowing within me once more.

That can't be the Vanessa I just saw. This one is so… majestic. God-like, even. Extended, straight-as-a-needle silver hair, five yellow necklaces, a flowing white toga, three golden halos above her head, skin as clear as day, brown sandals with a pair of white eagle wings on each, and a crown with a transparent, crystal sphere at the crest.

And there is something else in the picture. Five things actually. My friends. All of them. Z, D, Azilez, Griff, and Vizor, all with their eyes turned black. I cannot sense their presences at all.

"Now, bow down, worthless peasant, to Divine Neona!"

Chapter 44

Fated Face-off

"**Y**our cowardice knows no bounds, does it?" I cross my arms.

"Whatever do you mean? Aren't you going to mourn at the sight of your dead friends and brothers?"

"Please, don't make me laugh. Do you really think I wouldn't see what's happening here? Their life forces are inside you. It's the only reason you look like this right now. It's not your powers. So give 'em back before I rip them out of you!"

"I'd like to see you try!" Vanessa fires a bright-white laser in my direction. My skin bends like a wave pool.

I see flashes of flickering white light. It's Aria's spirit. She calls out to me. "Destroy her, V. Grind her into dust until nothing remains."

"Aria…" That's not what she wanted for Vanessa. But at this point, do I have another choice?

The white light wears off. I can see again, but I feel burnt all over. That light scalds like steam.

"A pity. I thought this would be more climactic. Oh, well. I'll just destroy Earth now. Or will you go into your divine form and do that for me?"

"See, that's the difference between you and me. You don't know how to control power. I DO!" The power of all 20 prophecies fills me once more: the power of the sun, the power of the shadows, the intensity of psychotic thoughts, and Neon's soul. All of it coming together under The Legend of V's banner to protect this world from anyone who threatens it! The internal soul barrier from Vanessa's illusion shatters.

"Well, then, I'll just let it loose!" She fires more lasers in all directions. Up, down, sideways, and everything in between. I'm forced to block the ones headed at Earth. If even one of them hits, it's game over. The Earth will be destroyed. And that's not something we can just bring back.

Luckily, my scaly wings can block all the lasers, so I don't have to tank them anymore. But there are so many! I have to get up close and personal so Vanessa fights me.

When my wings block the final laser, I let out one big flap and Vanessa gets caught in a pillar of flame. She's immobile! Now's my chance. I get close and slice at her with the edge of my right wing. The pillar subsides and she tumbles back. Her arms are glitching again. Her stolen powers are getting weaker!

"GrgRGgrgRGRghH! Why you…!" For the first time ever, Vanessa herself charges at me. I don't want to know what those glitch arms feel like, so I sidestep and back-kick her on her legs, sending her flipping upward. I meet her at the apex and skydive into her with all of my flaming body.

"Take this! SOLAR SUPERNOVA BLAST!" I lift my wings as high as I can, channeling all of the heat on my body to the tips. A great ball of fire the size of Earth forms over me. With one mighty flap, the ball volleys toward Vanessa.

"NOooOOO! Not like this!" She leans her head at the ball until the halos face it. An eerie-sounding black hole forms at the halos' base. The blast gets absorbed. She sends it back at me.

Since I'm not in front of Earth this time, I'm not afraid to dive under it, ascend, and fly-kick her to the heavens. She anticipates and meets me with her elbow. Our powers cancel out and we're reset to neutral positions.

She flies at me again. I use my wings to guard, but her glitch arms seep right through and get at me.

Dofqeioqnweflkfnoqiqoegbeuiqh0e9h835080rhe-b230238rh320rirjw0rewrh03rh239r3h30`32r9`23r r0239rh0234

So that's what it feels like being grabbed by a glitch. I'm flung at

Earth. Vanessa follows me. I resist the gravitational pull and fly, fists-first, at her. She doesn't hold back. We meet at the end of the exosphere. She swings with her left arm. I pull my head back. Then she leans her own head back and bops with mine.

"OW!" The ringing in my head isn't answered with high praise. I lose balance for a bit. Vanessa seizes the chance, charges her glitch arms with bright-white light, and hammer-arms me so hard that I orbit the Earth in seconds. Adsoifhqoiehq0e h91h3091h39031h4tn13e rqwe qerh1 34r81340r91h4r184r914r b3rehf0er1i32rh03rekfoew. When I re-volve back, she jump-kicks me with the bottom of her sandal and chases me down. But as she tries punching me again, I flip forward, cutting her forehead with my wings.

"OhoOhooHoHOHOhooOOOOO!" The cyber-crashing cry causes her face to revert to her glitch form too. "sO yOU liKe seeinG ME liKE ThiS? IS thAT iT?"

She rushes me again, but is blocked by Azilez and Vizor! In their chaos forms!

"Guys! How did you–?"

"The glitching, V." Vizor starts. "Every time a part of her becomes disjointed, one of us gets released."

"Then let's unleash the beast!"

"HELL, YEAH! I'VE BEEN WAITING FOR THIS! GET READY, YOU PSYCHO WITCH!"

"EhehehEHEHheheHhe!" Her laughs continue to grow creepier.

Azilez transforms her golden staff into a 20-foot frying pan. She bonks Vanessa's glitching head with it, only to lose balance and com-pletely miss her.

"FoOOOOL! I aM nOThiNg!"

"If only!" Vizor rushes in, spinning head-first with his blades out. Vanessa fires a lightning bolt at him. Vizor's blades absorb it and become electrically charged.

SHRRRRIING! Right across the torso! It glitches back to "nor-mal." Now only her legs, halos, and toga remain. At this point, though, the toga might as well be a washrag.

"GraGGhHHGAgrAgH!" Even the light that Vanessa fires isn't complete anymore. The next one she fires is just TV static. Azilez plans to tank it.

"NO! Don't!" I shoulder-bump her out of the way. Iadhfqoeh-r913hr013hr 013h4r19 gq90enf 4r3orbweugqd9fnsdlfoasd nfoqre g0q-etq; eqldghpqerig qelknq orh[4jt.34jbt'4t[4it[';4ot14[4t.

My consciousness is fuzzing. I'm not sure how many more of those I can take before I end up like her.

Before Azilez has the chance to say thanks, Vanessa is already in her face. Azilez tries using her rainbows to shield herself, but Vanessa just goes through them.

"Make way, coming through!" Z swings at Vanessa's legs with his putter. You know, the one from the putt he was about to make. "That's for stalling my tournament. Although the prize here is worth way more than some trophy."

"UGhHuguhuhguhgUGhu dioeo1rm3r390r 3r we0fe0jd…" Now she's just making random noises. It's not even laughter anymore. No one can understand her. I bet even she doesn't know what noise that is supposed to be.

The toga and the halos on top of her, by themselves, begin glitching too. Griff and D tumble in and accidentally tackle Z.

"Uhh… is she okay?" D holds his ears shut. He can't stand the noise.

"No, D. She isn't."

Five shining yellow objects eject from Vanessa. She returns to her human self, encased inside one giant prophecy.

Out from the recesses of space, a single Omoh sapien ship returns. Scrougholwer opens his cockpit and looks at all six floating tablets. "Finally. The remaking of the universe can begin. Plaplapla!"

Chapter 45

The Great War

EONS AGO - SCROUGHOLWER

"Cowards! Listen here! We are fighting for my dominion. My rightful reign on this miserable planet called Earth. Now, fight for me so that one day I might kill you all!"

"Hooooorrrraaaahhhh!" the army cries out. I watch from the height of a dry cliff, alongside my superior, Syzor. The one and only Syzor. The leader of the Omoh sapiens in our fight against the humans.

"They will invade us tonight! Be ready. Be ruthless. No one is to be spared!"

I sit in my tent at the head of the camp, alone, finishing my dinner. My silk white cape sits on the bare carpet Syzor just gave me.

"Vice chief Scrougholwer? Are you in here?" a feminine voice calls from outside.

"Yes, you may enter." I'm not like Syzor. I don't really rule with an iron fist, but I try to be authoritative when I can. "State your name."

"Sieelle, sir. I'm leading the defense shortly." A petite woman with pitch-black blades in her hair raises the folds of the tent and sits down on the hard rock.

"Well, what are you doing here? Should you not be at your post?"

"That's actually what I came to talk to you about. I'm not a very experienced leader. I'm not sure what to do. I've fought before, but never have I led. What do you think I should do?" She clasps her hands together.

"Leading is a gut instinct. I can't tell you how to lead."

"But, sir, please! I need assistance. If you cannot counsel me, can I at least have an assistant commander?"

"You know that's not up to me. All referrals go through Syzor."

"He'll just kill me if I tell him this! I don't even want to fight. This war seems pointless." She breaks down with her hands on her face.

There are some Omoh sapiens who skipped the whole "destroy everything" gene that the Devil gave to our kind. She must be one of them.

More and more of them have been coming to talk to me as of late. Maybe because they finally realized they'd actually have to get blood on their hands. That is a heavy burden to carry, I will admit. It's not for everyone. In my years of infantry, I've slaughtered many, but never really looked back. I guess you could say I'm a mix of the destructive Omoh sapien and the ones like this Sieelle here.

"Okay, listen. I understand your plea, and I will assist you. But it requires treason. Are you prepared for the possible consequences?"

"Anything to escape this war!"

"Very well. Run beyond the cliffs that Syzor and I were standing on top of earlier today. A lush green field waits there. Go a little farther, and you'll start to see hills. Caves exist on those plains, and they're largely uninhabited. You will be met by some of the others."

"Excuse me, sir. Others?"

"You aren't the first one to seek my assistance. Other traitorous kind-hearted folk have already escaped. They will guide you from there. Now go! I will inform Syzor that I have slaughtered you."

"Bless you, Scrougholwer! Bless you!" She recomposes, smiles, and runs off like the wind.

I hear marching in the distance. The humans are coming.

"Stand your ground, cowards!" Syzor sits on his throne, behind the thousands of lines of soldiers in front of him. I stand by his side, with my hands tightly clasped behind my back.

"Rrrraaaaahhh!" The humans cry out in the front of the line. They are greatly outnumbered. This should be a cakewalk.

Or so I think.

As the front is busy fighting, thousands of arrows come flying down from the cliffs above. They skewer our soldiers one by one.

"How is this possible, Scrougholwer? You told me the only path to the cliff is behind us!" Syzor looks about ready to destroy me.

"It is, sir! They must've scaled the cliff from another side."

"Grr! I'll deal with them myself." Syzor jumps off his throne and runs up the winding, rocky road behind us.

Thousands of our soldiers run past me to assist the king. Many of them are without commanders. At that moment, I realize I'd forgotten to replace all of the commanders I sent away. This carnage is my fault.

The battle subsides. We barely pull through. The archers at the top of the cliff are only forced back, and we suffer heavy casualties. I stand in front of Syzor, awaiting my punishment: the Evil Crossbow.

"It seems our vice chief has grown soft, cowards! Do you know what this means? The battle we nearly lost was ALL HIS FAULT."

"HOOO! HOOO! HOOO!" The remaining soldiers fly their fists in the air.

"Say your prayers, Scrougholwer."

"Why should I pray to the evil that is about to course through me?" I rebut.

"My, my! This defiance! I didn't know you had it in you. That's good to know." Syzor cranks the setting on the crossbow to the max.

Well, this is it. There's no way out for me.

PEEEEWWWWW!

… Huh? I'm still conscious? How? I thought… no! NO!

"Sieelle!" She lies on the rock, motionless. A pool of blood stains her entire back. She must have jumped in front of the crossbow just in time to save my life.

That's the last thing I remember before I got chopped in the neck.

Chapter 46

Salvation in Return
EONS AGO + A WEEK – SCROUGHOLWER

Ngh… where am I? Hell? No, it's not hot enough. A drop of water falls from above and into my right eye, prompting it open. My left eye follows. I seem to be in a cave.

Five Omoh sapien figures, all wearing scarves to cover their faces, appear before me.

"So you're up? That's a relief. Sorry if I hit you too hard." The one on the far left shakes his hand back and forth.

"Eh… wait. You're all the commanders I saved from the army, right?"

"Well, most of them." The middle one walks up. He's by far the tallest.

"A sixth came, but had a hunch you were in trouble when she saw five other commanders hiding here. She ran back to your aid, and, well… you probably know the rest."

"Oh. So that wasn't a dream."

"Afraid not. Sieelle is gone."

"How incredibly noble of her…" I almost tear up, but not quite. I've seen way too much already. Fighting with Syzor by my side is a constant gore fest.

"So, what now? Syzor will be after you, right? You're a criminal in the eyes of the Omoh sapiens."

"I suppose." I'm not really sure what to say. My neck still stings.

"Then let's all get out of here! They'll know where we are eventually."

"Eventually is now, maggots!" Syzor's voice booms through the cave. Five arrows from the Evil Crossbow skewer the friends that just saved me. "Well, now. I didn't expect you to be a coward. But alas, that's our kind. We're scum, and you'll be dying proof of that."

"So that's it then? You'll just kill the next problem you see?"

"What are you going on about, traitor?"

"If we're all scum, then why do anything? Why are we fighting? Let's just give up on Earth and find whatever other planet we want. There's less blood involved."

"BLOOD IS WHAT FUELS OUR KIND!"

"Says who? The Devil? Please."

"YOU ARE TO NEVER DISOBEY THE DEVIL. IT WILL DESTROY YOU IF IT HEARS YOU."

"It won't matter. You'll just shoot me anyway."

"Grr! I don't need this. Goodbye, Scrougholwer!" He shoots at me. Difqoeih83h103n0eht t1049t-1 4tn43ot t1-4to4tdk fnqowh ifgpo-q;egoq ;rgqe aosdifpqeone 4dioaeqdanfoqe. "What... what was that?"

"OnLY yoUR siLENcinG!" I raise my shaking hands. The souls of the five commanders Syzor just killed fly up into five tablets. Those tablets break off the stalactites, fall down, and reflect the arrow into Syzor's shoulder.

"AAAaaAHHHH!"

"SeEmS wE unDeRSTand eacH otHeR nOW. We'VE loSt thIS wAR. GoT iT? UnLEsS yoU WANt anoTHeR aRROw iN yoUR sHoULDer."

"FINE! But I get something too!" Syzor snatches the five new tablets and stuffs them in his blades. "I'll never give these back to you! HA!"

Chapter 47

Resistance Right on Time
330 YEARS AGO;
TREAH – SCROUGHOLWER

"And so, cowards, my reign here is over. I will now rest in my rightful place in the black ice, until I am called upon again. As proof of my reign as king, I shall take my blades in my hair, and display them in the royal hall for all to see. Syzor the Second, I pass my crown to you." Syzor the First speaks these final words before he preserves himself with black sleeping ice.

This is my ticket to creating a new universe. I still haven't forgotten what I set out to do so long ago: help the souls of the lost and wandering to find a place they can call home.

Syzor the Second embraces the Omoh sapien crown, and the crowd erupts. Vizor, his son, hides behind his royal cape.

"Get off!"

"O-okay…" Vizor twiddles his foot.

I sit at the base of the platform, waiting for the new king to walk down. "Congratulations, Syzor the Second. Inheriting the past king's name is no easy feat on Treah. Or, under it. You know what I mean." Yeah, Treah's not like Earth. The surface is near uninhabitable, so we build our cities underground.

"Much obliged, Scrougholwer."

"Please. If you need any assistance, I am willing to help, even in my retirement."

"Well, maybe I'll need help executing my plan to carry out the legacy Syzor the First left for me."

KekeKEkEkEkEke… just as planned. I rush to the castle guard.

"May I see the blades of my old friend before they are encased in glass for the rest of eternity?"

"Whatever, you old coot." The two guards throw the blades at me.

YesYesYESYESYES! Come to me, Starlight Prophecies! We shall renew this miserable creation we've been given. They enter my body like a spirit.

The castle is being remodeled to fit the next Syzor's liking. Not that it means much. Omoh sapiens don't really have personalities outside of "KILL, DESTROY, RAID!"

However, in recent years, the leadership of this planet has had to do something they… how do I put this nicely… despise.

"Syzor the Second? Are you in here?" The leader of the vampires, Count Dracula, looks like a fool wandering about in the redesigned castle.

"Up here, Mister Drac." Vizor waves from the railing in the castle. He smiles and waves his arms.

"Ah, Vizor, my boy! It's good to see you. Where's your daddy?"

"Right here, Dracula." The new king walks into the blue, carpet-lined hallway. He's finally finished putting on all of his attire. A little vampire reveals herself from behind Drac's leg. "My, my. Who is this?" Syzor kneels down.

"Uh… uhh…" The little vampire can't muster the words.

"She's my daughter, Hazy," Dracula introduces her.

Vizor scuffles over to her. "H-hi. I'm Vizor."

Hazy puts on a shy smile. "Uh… Hazy! Nice to meet you."

"Now, Vizor. You know the rules. You are to stay behind me at all times during these important meetings. This involves only Dracula and me. Understand?"

"Yes. Sorry, father." Vizor hides his face under his big hair and steps back.

"Now, then, how are things on Earth? Have you caused the humans any more trouble?"

"Not yet. We're still safely situated in Romania, living in isolation."

"Excellent. No one is to find out you are there. Things will be... difficult otherwise. Understand?"

"Yes, of course."

Come on! Get to the part about the eventual takeover of the Earth so I can sabotage it!

9rehro39r023r23   qe r[4[j4ptj14t4-t1489th104 t4l 0we perj09 qp4r4 p43j 43ih0e t34ptj4309jpewomfq ef qfqeqwe weof dnfo-qwef09443-9q4

"Unnghh!" I grasp my head in pain. The power of the Starlight Prophecies wears off suddenly. I can't spy on the meeting from my home anymore.

– What gives? You're supposed to obey me.

– No. You're too nice. We couldn't possess the man that helped us in our hour of need.

– What are you? Dense? I created you, and that means I command you. Now possess me. I must have the power to restart everything.

– You don't have that capability, even with us at your side.

– Of course I do. I was vice chief of the entire Omoh sapien race. I can handle anything.

– You are also the reason that we are not the dominant race on Earth. Only the vampires live there now.

– Nrrgh...! I can still make up for my mistake. I can create a new world. With all of you. Your newfound powers in your spirit form will be all I need to recreate this universe. I've been waiting eons for this. Please! I promised to help you, and I did. Now help me.

– There are no promises in insanity. We need to find a host who understands this.

– NO! Please. You're all I have left. I stayed alive all this time for you.

– We'll be back. I promise. Let that sink in for a couple hundred years.

The prophecies leave my front door, the planet's atmosphere, and disappear into the vacuum of space.

Fine. I was prepared for something like this anyway. I head into the meeting room, where my comrades wait for me.

"How have you all been?" I ask as I sit at the helm of the table.

My friends nearly tackle me with all of the things they have to say. I'm like their psychiatrist. These are all of the Omoh sapiens I've helped through my countless eons on Treah. This is how I've kept myself busy all these years. There's no way I would've just waited idly for so long. That'd be insane. I've been building an army, and now I think it's finally ready to storm the castle and take it for the sake of the helpless!

"Now, then, I think it's time, everyone. It's been a long time coming. Let's kick it!"

"The castle is ours for the taking," I say as I put on my chief's cape again. "Ready? CHAAAAARGE! Plaplapla!"

"Hrrrrrraaaahhh!" Since a resistance of this magnitude has never happened in Omoh sapien history, we outnumber the guards at the base of the castle and easily overtake them.

The raid rages on. Bit by bit, floor by floor, my army dwindles, staying behind to deal with the influx of guards being called in. I miss this rush! The feeling of being able to die at a moment's notice. The experience of sharing it with my comrades. And, best of all, the ability to lead!

I approach the throne room, ready to take on Syzor the Second. But the door is already open. "Hello?" How can someone have already gone in here? It was probably just Vizor.

"Glad you could make it, Scrougholwer." That's not Syzor's voice, but I can tell it's him from the back. What in blazes is going on?

"I'm here to take your castle?" At least that's what I think I'm doing. Ohh… my age is getting to me. Or is it something else?

A black-and-purple serpent spirit emerges from his feet and knocks me out with one tail swipe.

Journal Log #1: Well, there's good news and bad news. The good news is that my crew and I survived whatever that spirit was. The bad news? We were banished for invading the castle. For eternity. So now, I'm just going to sit back, relax, and explore the wonders of space with my friends.

And when the Starlight Prophecies show themselves again, I'll know. They've been inside of me after all. I'm a part of them.

Chapter 48

Star Light, Star Bright

"Well, I guess there are promises in insanity after all, eh?" Scrougholwer says. "You five came back." Is he talking to Vanessa's Starlight Prophecies?

"He's been this way for a long time, V." Vizor pats my shoulder. "Poor guy."

"And you even brought back Sieelle! Wow, I underestimated you. Plaplapla! *cough* *cough*."

"Hmm... interesting story, prophecies. So this is how it ends for me, huh?" Vanessa regains consciousness inside the giant prophecy. "Well, I better savor this moment, then. Ready, prophecies? Destroy him!"

The Starlight Prophecies fire off a beam so bright that it shatters the prophecies themselves and evaporates Scrougholwer. The power and dust scatter in all directions. "Hehe. Well, that's all the playtime I'm getting. I'm ready to go back now, V."

"Huh? To Earth?"

"Yup. Take me to my cell. I'm spending eternity in there after all. Inside this tablet, I can't do anything. It's made of a combination of Syrusima and rock material. It's indestructible. Go ahead. Hit it with your strongest attack."

With not much else to do except wonder, I conjure up another solar supernova blast and send it at Vanessa. Nothing. Not even a scratch from my strongest attack in my divine form. "Huh. You're right."

"Of course I am. Now, let's go. Home awaits."

"Uhh... okay. Let's go, guys."

"Sure?" Azilez is as confused as ever.

"Fine." Vizor has a sour taste in his mouth.

"What just happened?" D can't wrap his head around anything right now.

I think I get the limbo we're caught in. We just saw a living, breathing being evaporate from a light blast that could destroy worlds and barely reacted. It's like we're just waiting for it all to end so we can go home and finally get away from this horror we've found ourselves in.

We drop off Vanessa at Alcatraz. It was the slowest we'd ever moved in our extreme forms. It took an hour to get from the tree house to Alcatraz, and back to the tree house again. That's a trip that should've taken two minutes tops. But none of us can find the strength to do anything right now. I guess we're just... thinking, but I don't know.

Even before we walk into the house, the Dark Spirit courses through all of us, trying to make us feel physically better, but it's no use.

We arrive back at the tree house.

All of us come down with incredibly high fevers the day after. And a freezer for Vizor.

Chapter 49

Sicklings Scared for Life

My head…

"Hey, can someone pass me the ice pack?" I reach out to the sky as high as I can. Which is a grand total of half a foot before my arm gives up.

Vizor shivers at the thought of anything cold.

Azilez is drained from having to create an infirmary using her brush. She has extended the platform at the entrance of the tree house and created a small shack for the six of us to stay in, since we don't want to get our parents sick, just in case.

Our fevers are dangerously high, clocking in at about 105 degrees Fahrenheit. And Vizor's freezer is 53 degrees Fahrenheit.

– *Sorry, V. I told you I couldn't heal these kinds of things. You'll get through it. I'm sure!*

– *Honestly, I don't know.*

– *What are you saying? Of course you will! Your powers will help you through it.*

– *This isn't just some fever, Dark Spirit. Don't you get it? It's not some virus that did this to us. Our own minds did.*

– *That's insane!*

– *Exactly.*

The Dark Spirit can't find any more words of advice. – *Just know that I'm here for you, then. We're friends, right?*

– *Absolutely. Nothing will change that.*

– *Great to hear.*

– Can You get me an ice pack? I don't think anyone heard me.

– At once, V. The Dark Spirit leaves my body, but I feel no different.

"Uhhhhh… Vizor? You up?"

"S-s-s-s-sort of."

"What's the lowest a freezer can… be?"

"O-o-only f-f-f-fifty. I'll d-d-d-d-die past t-t-t-that."

"107 degrees is the human limit."

All of our parents barge into the door. Behind them, a team of doctors and nurses. Normally, we'd go to the doctor for this, but we're so frail right now that they had to come to us. So much for not getting our parents sick.

Candice is sweating bullets, worried about Azilez. She places two cool, moist hand towels on her forehead. She smiles in response. Candice bursts out crying and cradles Azilez's upper body in her arms.

"So what you're telling me," one of the doctors wants to clarify to my dad, Kal, "is that I have to feed junk food to this one here to get him better? And what qualifications do you have to bestow this information?"

My dad replies. "No one on this planet has the qualifications to treat an alien."

"The medicine we have should do the job better. Step aside."

"No, wait!"

"I-I-I-I-It's fine, Kal…"

"Vizor, no! The injections they'll give you could kill you. You need a different treatment."

"N-n-n----nn---n---n---no, I don't. None of us d----d-d-d----d--d-d-do."

"What are you talking about? If we do nothing, you'll just sit here and it'll get worse."

Vizor falls asleep.

Griff's mom and dad are reading him a children's book he's had since he was a toddler: *The Little Car that Could.* It's always something that cheers him up when he's down in the dumps. Griff is sleeping too, though. No one knows if he's listening to the story or not.

Even though there are six beds, D is cuddled in the same one as Z.

IVs, X-rays, a plethora of medicine, and scientific initiative. These are all things the doctors have at their disposal, and they still can't find anything wrong with us.

Chapter 50

Lightmare

Wait... why am I in another white field? Vanessa is trapped in Syrusima, isn't she? The Starlight Prophecies are gone. She can't use them anymore.

"Hello? Anyone here?" My cry echoes through endless space. Nothing. There's no one–

"V, THERE YOU ARE!"

"Ahhhhh! Oh, phew. It's just you, Azilez." I'm relieved to hear her booming voice and see her gleaming smile and paintbrush.

"Not just me."

Out of a nearby blue puddle, Vizor, Z, D, and Griff poke their heads out.

"Oh, V! C'mon, the water's great." Griff signals with his hand.

"How are you guys so calm? Do you realize the danger we could be in? This is Vanessa's home turf."

"Relax, V. This is a dream," Vizor reassures.

"How can you be so certain?"

"Watch. I want some chocolate ice cream." Vizor holds out his hand. From the sky, a scoop of brown ice cream stuffed with chocolate-bar bits splats on his hand. Vizor licks it down like a cat drinking milk.

I tilt my head, still finding it hard to believe that this is some dream.

"Forget ice cream. I want a sweet ride!" Griff throws both his arms into the air, splatting D's head. A bright-orange Formula One race-car lands, upside down, adjacent to Griff. He jumps out of the puddle and pushes it upright with all of his strength.

Now I know we're in serious danger. "Griff?"

"Yeah, what's up?" He's tending to the scratches on the car.

"Why did it take you so much energy to only tip over a car?"

Griff freezes, realizing what I mean. He tries entering his chaos form, but fails. "Oh, no. Our powers are gone!"

"RIGHT YOU ARE." Vanessa, in her divine form, thuds the ground.

"You!"

"THAT'S RIGHT. ME. AND THESE TOO." She reveals all 20 prophecies.

"Wait, how did you...?" Griff frantically searches his drenched backpack.

Vizor doesn't say anything but shakes his hair blades, hoping for the Shadow Prophecies to plop out. No such luck. Vanessa's prophecies are the real deal.

"GOOD LUCK BEATING ME WITHOUT THESE."

"I thought you said you had no more playing to do."

"PLaY TimE'S oVeR!" Her head glitches. It immediately reverts to normal. A yellow shockwave sends all of us careening back.

Everyone tries channeling their chaos forms, but can't.

"This isn't fair! There's no WAY we can beat you now!" Azilez pulls her hair.

"THEN GOOD RIDDANCE." Vanessa pounds the already-cracked ground with her fist. The resulting earthquake launches us. Vanessa flies up and smacks us with the back of her radiant hand. All of us tumble into each other, not able to do anything except take it.

"HAHAHAHAHAHAHA!" Vanessa rains down holy lightning and zaps each of us, only to throw us into the pond we were just in and zap the water. We're still conscious. We try getting up and running off, but Vanessa uses the light to materialize a giant yellow hand and catch us. She slowly brings us right to her beautiful face. "PARTING IS SUCH SWEET SORROW, SO WHY PART AT ALL? WE CAN STAY HERE FOREVER!"

Vanessa flings me into the electrically infused pool. She drops Griff to the ground below.

Vizor is head-butted. His entire face bruises. Vanessa winds up and chucks him on top of Griff.

She punches Azilez in the stomach repeatedly until she vomits and drop-kicks her out of sight.

Vanessa pounds Z and D's heads into each other until they bleed. Vanessa inhales deeply and blows a mighty wind from her mouth, sending them, along with myself, into the pool.

"COME BACK. I'M NOT FINISHED YET!" With the snap of her fingers, all of us are teleported back into her light-induced, giant hand. "I'D HATE FOR THIS TO STOP. AREN'T YOU HAVING FUN? A CLASH OF WITS AND A TEST OF PASSIONS! ISN'T IT ECSTACY FOR YOUR SOUL?" None of us can muster the strength to say anything. How can we? None of our souls are present. How can they be? They were all taken and stifled by the goddess before us. "AWW, NO REPLY? THEN I'LL FORCE ONE OUT."

The Vanessa-family mansion's entrance appears again, with the kitchen and the stairs and everything. Without us doing anything, we tumble up the leftmost staircase and crash into the last door in the corridor. The door takes us into the depths of outer space. We crash-land on Treah, in the royal castle.

Vizor is the first to stand. The gravity is inverted, so we're all on the ceiling's railings. Vizor touches his face, but immediately pulls his hand back. His face hurts too much. With the little sight he has, he spots two royal towels on the ceiling, grabs them, and applies them to Z and D's blood wounds. From the ground, volleys of medieval-looking weapons fly upward. With the last ounce of energy he has, he parries each weapon to make sure they don't harm the rest of us. "GRRRR! JUST KEEL OVER ALREADY!" Vanessa tilts over a lava bucket, releasing the molten mass. Vizor throws his blades at the lava. All of it is absorbed. The blades melt. New ones replace them. Vanessa snaps her fingers again. Vizor passes out.

We're in Van Gogh's *The Starry Night*. Azilez sniffs the oiled-on colors and swirled patterns and darts upright. She grabs her brush from her pocket and a lone painter's palette from the floor. Vanessa appears in the sky. She gently blows across the top of her blazing palm, melting the paint. Azilez dabs her brush in some oil paint and jumps into the flames. She strokes and swirls her brush across the floor, reapplying life to the burnt portions. The smoke from the fire forces her to cough. After all of the fire subsides, she still stands, painting away. Not for long, though. Vanessa clenches her fist and snaps her fingers. The lack of air renders Azilez unconscious.

We're all face down on some grassy tract. Griff moves his hand around. He touches a wheel and tilts his head up. We're all on a racetrack. Griff turns around, eyeing Vanessa in a monster truck. In an adrenaline rush, he throws all of us into the cockpit of a nearby Formula One, revs up, and takes off. Vanessa chases after, destroying much of the grass and track barriers in the process. Griff makes sure to drift at the corners to lose as little speed as possible. One slip could mean death by squashing. "YOU'RE MINE NOW!" Vanessa draws closer. The traction on Griff's tires is wearing off. He's got one good drift left in him. He barrels toward a wall. Vanessa continues to follow. At the right moment, Griff sharply turns the wheel, revealing a gas tank. Vanessa can't avoid it in time. BOOOOOOOOOOOOMM! Vanessa flies onto the charred grass, tearing parts of her toga. "THAT'S IT! I'VE HAD ENOUGH!" Vanessa snaps her fingers one last time. We're back in the white field.

She creates a bow using rays of yellow light, and loads it with six arrows from her quiver. I huddle all of my friends behind me. Vanessa fires.

"I've had enough out of you!" A furious white flare intercepts all arrows. It incinerates them on the spot. "Your madness ends here." A figure touches down onto the ground. It sends white debris into Vanessa perfect eyes.

The dust rises like a curtain. I can only see the back of the figure, but I can tell it's Neon from the toothbrush haircut. The white-hot flames in his hair seem to spire a mile high. Two pairs of rocket wings protrude from his back, with one massive fuel burner in between them.

"No way. How are you back? I turned you into fuel." Vanessa brushes off her toga.

"That may be, but that's just what this rocket needs to soar. And that's bad news for you. Vanessa, I still can't wrap my head around the things you've done to all of us these past couple of years. I don't know why you did them. I just know those yellow rocks of yours caused it all. I am sending you packing, along with all these stupid rocks!" Neon scrunches violently. He clenches his fists, igniting his back's burner.

"I set you free and this is the thanks I get? A hostile greeting and a threat? You've much to learn, mortal."

"Save it. You're wasting your breath." Neon's wings extend and he blasts off, headfirst.

Vanessa flaps her sandals' wings mightily, forcing her upward. Her five necklaces glow. A white hole is summoned, ejecting lightning bolts and stray asteroids everywhere.

Vizor thuds his hair blades into the ground, trying to give the six of us some sort of cover.

I'm not sure how much longer I can keep my eyes open.

Neon turns around and lets his back burner fire off a white and red laser at Vanessa. She hides behind her white hole. It sends the beam scattering. Thankfully, none of them is in our direction.

"That's quite the blast. It seems you have succumbed to the prophecies' strengths after all."

"You'd like that, wouldn't you?" Neon faces her, cold stone eyes vibrating. His voice shakes at the end. Vanessa tilts her head. "It's granny's suit! And the power of the entire Phantom Pipeline." Neon's hair subsides, along with the flames. He places his palm on the ground. The derpy spirits scatter throughout his body. His feet become rocket propellers. His fingers become steel blocks. The fuel from his burner emanates dark blue. Red wires connect his feet, legs, and arms.

"How very touching." The white hole cannot sustain itself any longer and collapses. Vanessa teleports up close, gut-chucking Neon. He scrambles to his propellers. Neon flies away, leaving dark rocket fuel for Vanessa to navigate through. He blasts across the side of her head, trampling her. She recovers and tries summoning another white hole. She coughs violently instead. "Wh-what have you done?"

"Painful? Good. Do us all a favor and just keep slowly killing yourself by breathing it in."

The prophecies align like a rope. She grabs on and is escorted out of the toxic cloud, which is headed at us now.

"R-run!" D tries getting up, but the throbbing in his head thrusts him down. He tries dragging us across the floor with him, but falls over.

With the last of her strength, Azilez summons six rainbow gas masks and places them onto our faces using her brush. She collapses, dropping her brush.

The clouds pass over us. We're unharmed. But Neon is relentless.

"Just take it in and die already." Neon keeps ejecting the poison from his burners. Vanessa cannot find more places to run. The sky and ground is totally covered in poison mist. She extends her arms out to her sides, fists clenched. The 20 prophecies surround her, creating an airtight barrier. "Wait… no. No. No!" Neon realizes that he's played himself. He doesn't have any technology that allows him to avoid the toxicity. And since it's everywhere, he can't run from it. Eventually, his lungs force him to inhale a giant gulp.

Instantaneously, the wires holding him together combust. The wings on his back malfunction. He coughs out blood, but the clouds make it so foggy to see that the rest is a blur.

Some time passes, and the clouds subside. I look in Neon's general direction. There lays a blue puddle of slime.

The prophecies crumble. Vanessa is still in her divine form, but she looks drunk. She's wobbling aimlessly. She even trips over her toga. I see a chance to claim the prophecies. I crawl, mask still on head, toward her general direction. Vanessa holds her hand up. Several particles of light enclose to create a regal bow and six arrows. I turn back to see all of my friends still unconscious.

With the short nap I had, I regained some strength to stand and trot. I just have to get to the prophecies before she fires. That's all. C'mon,

I can see victory! It's literally right in front of-

All six arrows pierce through my stomach.

"Hahehaheha. Gotchyoo." Vanessa falls, face-first, unconscious.

The trauma throws me to my knees. The adrenaline rushes to my arms to prevent me from falling further. I toss myself to my side. Some blood seeps out my back, but because the arrows are still inside me, it's not much.

Vizor regains consciousness. "...Mgghhh. Huh? V? V!" He tries rushing to me but can't stand. He crawls over.

"Don't worry, Vizor. Arrows way stronger have pierced through me." I recall the Evil Crossbow. That one planet-sized arrow stung a thousandfold more than these. "But, we made it."

"What do you mean?"

"You screwed up now... Vanessa." I point at her. She regains consciousness. The toxic effects seem to have worn off. Her face's color reverts to normal. Just in time to reveal her grand mistake.

"What are you blabbering about?"

The arrows' energies mask the pain. "These arrows have our powers in them. And the prophecies'."

"NO! NO, THEY DON'T!" She panics.

I gulp. My body absorbs the arrows and my wounds heal. I grab Vizor and jump in front of my friends and brothers. "Let's get our souls back!"

"NEVER!" Vanessa grabs her bow and fires again. I jump, back-kick, and flames spew from the tip of my shoe, melting all of the arrows. I burp out yellow clouds. Rain and thunder ensue. Divine V is back in action!

The multicolored flames from Vizor's chaos form transfer from his head to his entire body. His eyes become golden, and he grows three layers of hair blades out of his back, which double as a weapon and wings.

Griff's hair grows to an incredible length. It becomes bright-orange. The jet-engine energy that came out of his hair during his chaos form now emanates from the bottoms of his feet. His eyes become dark-silver.

Azilez's dress from her chaos form grows even larger. It has seven layers. Each one is colored to match the order of a rainbow. The twisted golden staff doesn't appear. Instead, an actual rainbow arcs behind her, held together by two black thunderclouds that constantly follow.

Z grows two pairs of black eagle wings. His hair becomes white, and a white-hot, giant golf ball orbits him. His eyes turn sky-blue.

THUMP… THUMP… THUMP… Sometimes, D tells people to be one with nature, but I would've never imagined that he'd become nature. His skin and limbs transform into the base of a sequoia, his hair turns into tree leaves, his pickaxe is now a giant, black scythe, and D himself is ten-feet-tall and has slime-green eyes.

Vanessa fires six more arrows. D deflects them with his arm. Z points directly at Vanessa. His orbiting golf ball chases her. Vanessa flies around to avoid it, but Azilez grabs and chucks her. Azilez throws her hands forward, commanding two lightning bolts and a rainbow beam to strike Vanessa. Just in time too. The golf ball finds her.

BOOOOOOOOOM!

Vanessa lands with her knees on the floor.

"Give up, Vanessa." Z descends in front of her. All of us follow behind him.

"Hehehehehehe… HAHAHAHAHAHA! UGGWWAAHHADf-nieoqeoq9039 23jr123032"s snnD.///DANDFQIWEd;;g."

She slams her fists into the floor. The white field crumbles. Vanessa becomes a computer glitch again. She grows exponentially, too big to keep track of. We fly away, but the static spreads too quickly.

I don't know where she'll send everyone if she gets us, but wherever it is, at least I know my friends and family will be safe.

"Go!" I flap my wings once, creating a burst of wind that launches my friends and family.

"Wait, V…!"

I open my eyes to an apocalyptic scene. A large, brick building with a bell is burning to the ground. The thunder's rolling, the lightning's cracking, and the rain's pouring. The surrounding black hills are all blazing. It is difficult to distinguish anything.

Except when the lightning cracks.

ZAP! I can see an outline of Vanessa. Her body is only white, and no other features can be made clear anymore, except a smile with chainsaw teeth and twitching, yellow eyes.

"You'Re a BraVE SouL to FaCE mE AlonE!"

"I won't give you the satisfaction of toying with anyone else for any longer!"

"ThAt's FinE. aLL I nEEd Is OnE tOy, anyWaY."

"I won't let you."

"ThAt's WhAT theY aLL sAid."

All of the fire in the surrounding area glitches out. Sparks fly, light constantly flickers, and my depth perception is distorted.

Someone leaps at me. I assume it's Vanessa. I swing with all my might. Vizor blocks my attack.

"V, what are you doing? It's me!"

"Huh? Vizor? But I saved you guys! I flung you away to spare you the trouble."

Another person chokes me from behind.

Ieoe3r24 2903rj p2rmepwfm[w'f;a f.qewfqefqe jpr er02920.

Yeah, that's Vanessa. HA! I kick Azilez into the ground.

"OW! What was that for?"

"Wait, I didn't mean–" THUD. Griff hammer-fists me into the ground.

"Not cool, V!"

"I don't understand. How are you guys here? You should be safe, away from Vanessa's clutches!"

"tHAt's beCAuSe ThEy aRE." All five of them leap onto me and become one glitch. "BuT yoU AreN'T." Vanessa is trying to fuse with me like the Dark Spirit would.

CHCHCHCHHCZZZHCHCHCHCHZZZ!

"No! I won't let you!"

"WhY fiGHT iT? We'Re aLL pUpPeTs tO thE STronG. We KnEEl

bEfoRe thEiR pOinTinG HaND. anD HeRe Is MInE. BoW dOWN TO thE trUE ChosEn OnE!" I fight with every fiber of my divine being. The tension becomes so intense that lightning shoots out of Vanessa's mouth. My divine form's flames grow brighter. "yOU AnD I ArE noT So DifFeReNT. We BoTH pUShEd aSidE oUR frienDs to Get hERe."

"Did we?"

"HuH?"

"NOW!" Griff, Azilez, Vizor, D, and Z jump in from behind the flames. D grabs Vanessa. She can't break free. He flings her into the hill below.

Vizor throws his grappling hook at Vanessa. It latches on, and he flings her up to the cackling sky. The lightning zaps her.

"idhqoe9130r 13 3r3223rkwi2999999999!"

Vizor slices at her with repeated blade strikes. He ends with a forward punch.

Azilez follows where she's going to land. Her rainbow catches Vanessa. Z flies in and swings at Vanessa, sending her upward.

Finally, I leap into the sky. I flip forward, leg pointing out. "It's over." My mighty axe kick sends Vanessa into the building's bell. The sound oscillates so quickly that the illusion shatters. And so does Vanessa.

"AAAAAAAaaaaaaAAAAHHHHHHhhhhHHHhhH-HH! NOOOooooOOOO! BuT I... I... UUuuuuuuuuUURRRR-RAAaaAaAaaaaHHhHhHHhhHHhgggGGHHHhhhhHH----DIQE93 31kdho3 REMsssdefzdfgc dsfwe qqqfffas sal dk LKxd;alqwqorn lsj W xxswafedddsxccvs.,,"[111p3k43p4moE .39R013R P /E'ER[Q R998 &*)#))@@@*#HILN O3IO12 1LM 1 JWK283OL;']Q]]Q=L=+++M-FAOEP 3MRL13 RL3.DLSP flqmelfqo dw;omdasdmwSOmwoqw;m :Modw --"

Chapter 51
Free Will at Last

'm afraid to open my eyes. I have no idea how that last battle happened, or how Z, D, Azilez, Vizor, Griff, and I ended up on the same plane of thought. Let's take this slow. Right eye, open... oh. We're back in the tree-house infirmary. I open my left eye. Hey, my fever's gone! I feel great!

"Hey, V's finally up!" Griff greets me with an arm around my shoulder.

"Glad to see you made it back too." Vizor walks up to my bed, cross-armed.

"So I'm not crazy. It wasn't a dream. You were there in that white space with me?"

"DUH! No WAY we'd let you fight that psycho by yourself." Azilez has a skip in her step and a brush in her hand. Everything seems to be going back to normal. Thank goodness.

I remember bleeding heads. "Where are Z and D? Are they okay?"

"Don't worry! We're fine. And no signs of blood anywhere." Z is lying down on the bed next to mine. D pops out from beneath the covers.

"Did you see that, V? I was as strong as a giant sequoia!"

"Yeah, I saw that!" D and I get out of our beds, high-five, and exchange hugs. Everyone piles in. We all need hugs after what we just went through.

"Awwwww!" My mom walks into the infirmary. "Let me go get my camera."

"Scatter!" Vizor yells.

"Ahhhhhh!" We run out of the room in different directions. Some of us go to the tree house, and some of us go to the yard below.

"Aw, come on, guys. Just one." My mom comes back with her phone.

Vizor throws his hair blades like a boomerang at my mom's hand to knock the phone out. She ducks. "Vizor! I need thi–" BONK! On the way back, the blade handles hit the back of my mom's camera, breaking it. The blades return to Vizor, who slowly walks away, hoping no one noticed.

There is actually one other thing I want to make sure, just in case. "Griff? Vizor? Are the prophecies back?"

"Oh, right! That's what I forgot to do. Yeah, V. They're back. I gotta tell them that they can talk again. I told them to shut up at the Space Garden."

"That was probably for the best. Hopefully they just slept through most of it."

"Yes, the Shadow Prophecies are in my blades once more, safe and sound."

"Whew… that's a relief. Though I wonder how that white field thing happened, even after Vanessa was trapped inside that Syrusima-infused prophecy."

"I have a theory." Z raises his hand. Oh, boy, here we go. Hopefully this'll be better than that time he tried finding our way back to the Space Garden from Arsm. "Vanessa's powers turned sentient. They became her psychotic will. In essence, extremity defines a psychotic state. The powers she abused began controlling her. Our minds tried comprehending psychotic strength too, but couldn't. That's the reason we were all sick. Psycho attitudes spread like the plague. At some point our minds just turned off, trying their best to face whatever obstacle came our way. And y'know what? They did a pretty darn good job. For all we've been through, we tried our best to save the Earth. And everyone involved in Project Mutant. While we didn't have much control in that last bit, we tried what we could. And that's all we can really be satisfied with."

"… Wow, that's really deep. Not gonna lie, I didn't think you had that in you, bro." I pat him on the back.

"Thanks for having your utmost faith in me, bud."

"Noooo problem." I try giving him a noogie. I don't do a very good job.

"Nah. Let me show you how it's done!"

"Nononononononono! Get away from me! Ahhh!"

DING DONG!

Was that the tree house doorbell? It was. There's someone there. Looks like the mailman.

"Letter for… Z? Is it?" He's confused by the one-letter name.

"Oh, yeah. That's me."

"Well, here you go." He whistles down the ladder and walks along the sidewalk to the next house.

"What is it?" Azilez asks.

"It's from the tournament I was just playing in!" He tears it open, not really preserving the envelope. "It reads: 'Dear Z, Thank you for assisting in the saving of the city of San Francisco. We are much obliged and would like to express our gratitude. You are invited to play sudden death with the other leader, Harriet, today at 4 pm sharp!'"

"Well, what time is it?"

"3:45!" Candice calls from inside. "You crazy kids get a move on!" She throws Z's clubs from her room's window. Z dives and catches them.

"Thanks, I think," Z calls out to Candice.

"Anytime, love. Now go and kick that frilly chick's butt!"

"My car's got room for six. Let's ride!" Griff clicks on the car keys in his pocket. His orange hovercar appears before us. We all hop in, three in the front and three in the back. Because of the absurd speed the car is capable of reaching, we make it to the course in about five minutes. We unload Z's bag from the trunk, give him his cap, and send him off. We wait a few minutes before heading to the spectator's trail along the first tee, where Wellington is waiting for us.

"Well, it seems it has come to this. The final competitors battling for the gold in a sudden death." He shakes his head so much that he messes up his moustache.

"And we're takin' home the trophy, bub!" Azilez sticks her tongue out.

"My, what animosity. We'll let the competitors decide who is allowed to gloat."

"Fair enough." Azilez backs down.

Meanwhile, on the tee.

"Ladies first." Z flicks his wrist open.

"Why, how gentlemanly of you." Harriet drops her bag on the floor and goes up to hit her ball. THWAT! Right into the rough.

Z now goes to tee up.

I'm just glad I can see this sight again. I never thought I would at many points throughout this past adventure, if I can even call it that. It was more like surviving, hoping and waiting for the right opportunity to do anything within our control. Most of our time in the Space Garden – the Phantom Pipeline, facing Commander Rod, and especially with Vanessa – felt out of our control, but maximizing our opportunity during the parts that were in our control are the reasons we come out on top.

And the reasons we can live to fight another day.

PING! Right down the middle.

NEVER MISTAKE THE MEANS WITH THE END

www.thelegendofv.com

[f] The Legend of V
[▶] Varak Kaloustian
[𝕏] @KaloustianVarak

www.ingramcontent.com/pod-product-compliance
Lightning Source LLC
Chambersburg PA
CBHW051249250626
47155CB00009B/3232